Absorbed

Absorbed

Joanne Silver

Rev. date: 04/10/2019

To order additional copies of this book, contact:
Xlibris
1-888-795-4274
www.Xlibris.com
Orders@Xlibris.com
794416

Contents

Love

Inspirational

Shituations

Trauma

Being a Woman

Being a Man

Seasons

The water is deep, but you are deeper. I am here to take the burden and allow you to shine.

—Ma

Introduction

We absorb so many wonderful things in life from the moment we are born. The only thing we can do is absorb. Absorb and learn.

We immediately learn that when we cry, we are heard. We are immediately given attention. We absorb language. We absorb actions and play. We absorb sun. We absorb lessons. And sometimes, we become absorbed in the lives of others and their problems.

It's like my brain is exploding with thoughts, ideas, and solutions. I want to share them with the world, but the scariest part of all is that I'm not sure if my thoughts, ideas, and solutions are supported with evidence or validity. I am screaming on the inside with this burning desire to help, help everyone around me, and there is a term for this. It is called codependency. I am so focused on trying to control and rule everyone's lives into this vision I have for the perfect world.

I've compiled tips—lessons—stories and created this book in order to share them with the world. Life is such a beautiful thing we have been blessed with, and I love the lessons I've learned, the pain I have felt, and the healing I've done. I love the people in my life and their contribution to my strong spirit. Thank you to everyone around me, supportive and not supportive, loving and not so loving. Either way, you have helped shape and mold this now published author. ☺

Absorbed in other people's problems, they didn't
have time to identify or solve on their own.
—Melody Bettie (codependent no more)

Dedication

It's what you do to me.

To the girl who lifted me up from depths of the unknown, the one who, from the very beginning, has inspired me to go above and beyond and to reach for my wildest of dreams.

Someone once told me that if I am setting the example for the woman I'd love for you to be, I have nothing to worry about. This statement reigns true above all else. I know this because I have watched women follow their mothers in so many ways, positive traits and negative. I could tell you how to live and watch it backfire, or I could be the first and most important example for you.

With this book, you will forever understand how I have transformed year after year, month after month, and day after day, all thanks to the people and experiences I was able to absorb and learn from. You will understand how and why I have decided to be the person that I am today, the ways that I have chosen to mother you, and the ways that I have chosen to love the people around me.

Just days after you were born, I could see that you have the eyes of a learner. It's so natural to you.

I can only hope that you will take this book and fully understand your mother, in and out, good and bad. My intention with every accomplishment, failure, and step is to create an environment for you to be the best possible human that you could ever be. I will always be proud of the choices that you make if you make those choices with your whole heart.

You have been *my* whole heart and *my* whole reason for every choice, including this book.

I would like to include an important piece of advice for you, my daughter: please always forgive, always love, and always be kind. Not everyone learns this or understands this, but everyone needs love, forgiveness, and kindness.

Be that little piece of it all everywhere you go.

Self-Awareness

The Little Pink Pill

Ever since I could remember, I had always felt the urge to help others. I could remember being in kindergarten, I had already made a best friend. I'll call her Shelby. Shelby was my very best friend, and I had certainly grown a love for her even in my youngest years of life. I was five years old when Shelby missed her first day of school. I was sad and alone. I had grown so close to her I never had time to become friends with any of the other kids in my class. I grew worried, and the worry grew when my teacher had let me know that Shelby would be out for another day because she had a stomach virus. My immediate thought was I need to help. That night while my family was enjoying a lovely meal, I snuck off to the restroom and shut the door behind me. I climbed my little body on the bathroom sink and scrummaged through the medicine cabinet. I found the tiniest pill I could find because—hello—we were only in kindergarten; I couldn't imagine us being able to swallow anything much bigger than the one I had in the palm of my hand.

The following day was awful without her. *But just one more day, and she will be back in school,* I reminded myself. I skipped through the day the best I could. Today was the day she was coming back, and I was so excited. Upon arrival at school, I was so sidetracked from focusing on anything going on around me, and I had tunnel vision. I looked for Shelby. It wasn't long until I had spotted her.

"Shelby!" I exclaimed. "How are you feeling?" She returned a smile and responded that she was feeling okay.

I pulled her aside and handed her the tiny pill, and what do you know? It was pink! Shelby's favorite color. I was a people pleaser from the very beginning. Please tell me how grateful you are, Shelby. Tell me how I am the greatest friend any little girl could ever ask for.

At such a young age, I wasn't sure of the function behind my desire to please and my desire to care for others and cater to their needs and wants. I just knew it was an impulsive desire that needed to be fulfilled.

Anyway, let's cut the short story shorter. I gave Shelby the pill. She smiled, walked away, and continued with her day. The next thing I knew, I was having a meeting in the office with my teacher, the principal, some other important people, and my mom. Helping, caring, and loving led me here. The principal's office was on the verge of suspending a mere five-year-old girl.

This is the moral of the story: we care and love to the extent of negative consequences.

This is just the earliest point in my life where I can recall caring so much and trying so hard to help someone, and it ended up hurting me in the long run. It is damaging to learn something so important at such a young age. Of course, we want to care about those around us, and we want to love them with no concerns for the repercussions, but we need to be more cautious along the way. We need to be more concerned with ourselves. If we are not whole or we are not completely supportive or loving to ourselves as well as aware of some of the consequences that may come with our choices, we will continue to end up hurt.

It has been twenty-two years since that occurrence. I no longer know or speak to Shelby; however, I am still very much so absorbed and wrapped up in the lives of those I love and care about. I've been this way for years. I've burned my hand on the stove that others were cooking their own meals on just trying to help. I've hurt myself in more ways than I can count feeling the pain of those I love.

I tend to forget we are all walking our own paths, and regardless of the amount of compassion I feel for others, it's best for me to learn to walk my own path and let others do what they will because that is going to happen anyway. There are just some things and people that are out of our control.

Some of us have grown accustomed to feeling as though because we love someone so much and because we care so much, when those emotions are not reciprocated, it becomes *their* fault that we feel pain.

I am not trying to teach you how to live. There are millions of people who think they have the keys to living a happy and peaceful life, and for this reason, there are so many self-help books. I don't have the answers.

All I know is all that I've learned something in every phase in my life. I'd just like to share them with you in hopes that they can help you in the ways that they've helped me.

I have been a product of my own journey in life. I am learning every single day how to understand the human mind, not only for my career, but also for the well-being of my own mental health. I also work hard every day learning, reading, and trying to understand human behaviors so that I may someday be in the best position to pull others out of their sadness. I would love to help people identify the root of their issues and help them rise above them. With this book, I'd like to take you on my journey as well as the journeys of people that I have loved, cared about, and experienced. Maybe I've absorbed lessons from their stories, maybe I've absorbed compassion for their pain, or just maybe I just could have been absorbed in their lives in general. I am thankful for the lessons, I am thankful for the pains, and I am thankful for my overwhelmingly huge heart that has compelled me to become empathic and in tune with others' needs. No matter what path I've been choosing to take for all the years leading up to this one, I have finally decided to take a different route. This new route includes a whole ton of *self*. The time now has come to focus on *self*.

Watch Your Mouth

Over the years, we have been cursing ourselves more than any other person could ever do to us. We joke and fear that women around us are doing bruja stuff on our lives, causing our lives to forever be doomed and bring us nothing good. In the morning, when we wake up and the coffee we are making just so happens to spill across the entire counter, our first thought is "It's going to be one of those days." In this very moment, we are already setting the tone for our day—we throw those thoughts into the universe, and they hear us loud and clear. Walking to our cars, we realize we have locked ourselves out of our houses and don't even have our house keys on us. Our next thought or even this time the frustration has caused us to say aloud to ourselves, "This day can't get any worse." The universe responds, "LOL! What do ya know? Ending the day, you could not have had a worse day than the one you claimed would be terrible." What we think is what will be. I have learned this the complete hard way. For years, I would say stupid-ass shit like "Why me?" "Just my luck!" "Fuck my life," "If it isn't one thing, it's another," "When it rains—" Nah, stop that. When it rains, a beautiful rainbow pops up soon after!

You truly *cannot* afford to put all this negative shit out into the universe. Your mind is your semiautomatic gun. Fuck that, it is your bazooka. It is your most powerful weapon. I'm sure there are other weapons much stronger. Imagine your mind as whatever that weapon may be. I am less experienced in the weapon field, so I guess my mind is a bazooka. Either way, it has the power to alter life-changing events in your life. Understanding this is a practice. You won't stop thinking negative shit overnight, and you won't stop speaking negatively right away. I used to have the mouth of a trucker, like "fuck this," "fuck that," "fuck him"—you get the point. Clearly from my writing, you can tell that I have not completely

4

dropped this specific kind of vocabulary, but I have certainly learned to limit it where it counts. I work with children in a childcare setting, and the last thing I need is for the little kids to go home saying I was the one who taught them to use to word *fuck* at two years old. I didn't stop using the word; I just started to spell it out. Point is, I was able to learn to filter it in a way that was more suitable for my environment. Well, people, the life we live is our environment twenty-four seven, and I'd like to think we care enough about it to limit the possibility of creating our own negative events.

Imagine if we could change our lives and the way we live simply by changing the way we think or the things we say. For me, I have found that once I started changing the things I said or thought, my life started to adjust to the positive things I would think. Now this was not an easy process, and it certainly took time, but I started to do this aggressively. My best friend taught me to repeat "cancel, clear, delete" whenever I slipped up with a negative thing to say, and I truly found this to be helpful in remembering that as long as we remember to go back and imagine ourselves erasing these thoughts or sayings, we could still work on positive words daily. It's not like we're failing if we slip up; we're continuing to learn each day that nothing and no one is perfect and, despite the setbacks or mistakes, we are still growing.

Gratitude vs. Attitude

The ways my life has changed since I started practicing gratitude, I can only attempt to explain it, but how beautiful and amazing it is. This is one of the main things I'd love to share with you all.

I worked at a family-owned restaurant. I was soon after recognized by management for the simple acts of gratitude I practiced and would try to instill in the other servers. I'd write notes for the girls to keep in their money books to remind them to be thankful for every tip, every smile, and every nice table they had the opportunity to serve. This is easier said than done, I'm aware. I know it can be hard to bust your ass for a table and only receive a 10 percent tip, but still, be thankful.

Yes, I want you to practice gratitude for everything, big or small. When we practice gratitude and when we are thankful for life in general and everything it brings, an abundance of things will soon begin to flow into our lives. Not only that, it is much healthier mentally to be thankful than to be upset. When we spend our entire day upset over a small disappointment, it begins to take away all the amazing blessings we could be set to receive. Stop blocking your blessings by being ungrateful.

I created a list of wishes, kind of like a regular Christmas list, but this one pertained to *life*. I imagined the things I'd want in life, and instead of saying "I hope" or "I wish" or "I want," I'd thanked the higher being (or whatever higher power you believe in) for these things because my faith in achieving them is so sure and so strong. I know that if I leave any room for doubt, I am already setting myself up for the failure.

Sweep that shit under the rug, erase doubt, and believe in yourself. Setbacks, hurdles, speed bumps—the road always has a clear destination, and you *will* get there.

It's Already Yours

It's a real cliché thing to say "anything you want can be yours." I am, however, a strong believer in this. Anything you want can be yours! These words—*manifesting, envisioning, vision boards*—all these methods of attaining your goals and dreams are very real, and they work like magic. However, I promise you they will never work for you unless you truly believe in them. Whatever you need to do to become a believer, please do that, and watch the path of your life begin to move and shift for the greater. Some of the tips I can provide is just to remind yourself daily that you are thankful for the things you want because you <u>know</u> for a fact it is already yours. I do not care what it is; tell yourself it's yours. Just please don't imagine a specific significant other that you know damn well isn't going to happen because that's where creepy behaviors start to freak people out. This is something that would be called manifestation, and if you've never heard of it before, I am here to tell you this word and these ideas work like magic.

Please do not lose hope in this act. It is so crucial to remember we can change our lives, and if we manifest negativity and hope for good, it will never be good enough. Manifesting does not at all involve the word *hope*—to me, the word *hope* signifies part negativity and a little positivity. Certainly, hope does not represent enough positivity or belief in order to manifest our greatest desires. When we say things like "I hope so," this does nothing but confirm that you are unsure of the outcome. Stop saying "You hope," "You wish," and other phrases like these and start confirming and claiming the shit you want. Period.

I'll never believe a person is truly believing in themselves or manifesting positivity if I am constantly hearing them use phrases like the ones mentioned previously. Your life only starts to get better when your mind does. I have been focusing on this practice for years, and only recently have I started to be consistent with it. Don't get me wrong; there are still times when I find myself in this big negative Nancy mind-state, and I can't seem to get my head out of my ass in a bad way. I literally feel like shit. I will resonate all the negative things that could possibly ever happen to a human being and just visualize these things happening to me. Bad fucking idea! Try with all your strength, like lifting weights for the first time, and push and push yourself until those thoughts are completely out of your head. These thoughts and ideas and patterns of thinking are only a recipe for disaster. I can't sit here and dismiss your feelings, but I do understand we are sometimes faced with real-life hardships, and getting out of our negative mind-state is close to what seems to be impossible. However, what we need to remember is, the healing process is just that, a process. This means they are baby steps—less than baby steps, they are baby thoughts, and they will start to help you gain control of your life again. Start by practicing the idea of replacing one negative thought with three things you're thankful for. If initially this doesn't help, increase your list to five or ten. If it still doesn't work for you, then continue to keep thinking of whatever it is that makes you happy and really try to train your brain to stay on the bright side no matter how hard you must fight with it. It can play tricks on you, so reverse the role and do the same.

Solitary

Find peace in solitude and share silence with yourself. Make your time alone a priority, for this is the only way you get to know yourself on a personal level.

How disproportionate the way this works—we spend our whole lives with ourselves and yet still do not understand ourselves until we take the time to. It is damn near unattainable when we are so focused on the rest of the world—friendships, family, relationships, and everything else that has nothing to do with you.

Your individuality cannot be created or nurtured when you're not setting aside that time to do so. Unearth yourself from the surface. Bring to light what you love about yourself the most. Uncover the person you are continually living with. Once you experience and appreciate the satisfaction and elevation of your soul's vibration by practicing unattended time with yourself, you will long for more. It's healthy. It's necessary.

Coincidence Does Not Exist

Not everyone believes in the power of the universe or any other higher power you want to consider, but there is a higher power. Coincidence does not exist. We are living in a world where we are attracting the things we think, and if this has never happened to you, then you're the type of person who believes in coincidence. There is nothing wrong with those kinds of people, and I am not trying to sway you to think otherwise. (Okay, maybe I am.) There is a higher power; whether it's God you believe in, the universe, Buddha, or any type of religion you follow, there is always a force behind every single event. I have tried to be as open-minded as possible in learning new ideas and philosophies throughout this wonderful life, and one thing that has shown me actual results is believing in God and the way he maneuvers the universe to work for us. I believe in angels, spirit guides, and many other supernatural forces. I like to believe there are good qualities in these supernatural forces, and I believe they aren't always trying to claw the skin off our asses while we sleep, like in a horror film.

Have you ever randomly thought about a person, and then *boom*, they're calling you? Have you ever mentioned a person you have not seen in years, and then *bam*, you run into them at the grocery store? These are not coincidences. This isn't a book on chakras, but if it were, I'd have a whole lot to say as I have recently started my journey on becoming more aware of my own chakras and the way they work in my everyday life. The short of the subject is this: We all have seven chakras. They start from the bottom of our spinal cord to the top of our head. The root chakra is red; this is the bottom tip of our spinal cord, and this represents our sense of feeling or being grounded. The sacral chakra is orange; this represents our sense of wellness, sexuality, and creativity. The yellow is solar plexus—good for our ego and sense of self, empowerment, and self-awareness. Our heart Chakra is green; it represents our ability to give and accept love. The throat chakra is blue; this chakra helps us become great communicators and listeners. Are we speaking our truth? The third eye is indigo; it focuses on intuition and insight. The crown chakra focuses on our spiritual awareness; this can be represented by purple or violet and sometimes even white. When this chakra is balanced, or open, we have a good sense of spirituality. We're open-minded when it comes to this topic, or we have a good connection with the spiritual world.

Everyone has the power to be intuitively inclined, and this is called an open, or balanced, third-eye chakra. This is what I believe. There are other ways to see it, but if you're interested in learning about the chakras and the idea of learning how to open and balance them, this is a good place to start. Just to learn briefly about mechanisms to help you focus on opening these chakras if they happen to be closed, or blocked, research yoga positions and foods to eat in order to help you. There are also online tests to take that I feel are pretty good at helping you identify where your chakras are. That's as far as I'm going to get into the topic of chakras. I'm certainly no expert—currently learning all this myself too.

Just try to remain conscious of your intuition and really pay attention to the fact that this ability is truly a blessing and can only be enhanced with practice and faith. Just as the power and the law of attraction have stated, we attract what we think, and sometimes, we think what we attract. It goes both ways, and therefore, it is so crucial for us to constantly tread carefully and be conscious of the poisonous thoughts we are feeding our minds with.

You're given more than enough chances in life to restart your brain. Like an old gaming system that shuts down and freezes, turn that shit off, take some deep breaths, and start over.

Stop Talking the Talk

Right. Absolutely right. For the longest time, I kept talking about this book I have coming out. The only problem was that, day in and day out, I would never sit down and write. Words danced around in my mind, climbing in then escaping out, never to be remembered again. Weeks passed, I had not one page done. Months flew on by and still barely a chapter complete. I was talking to a friend one day, and I had mentioned, "Hey, I have this book coming out soon. Hope you'll make it to my launch party." He responded, "I don't want to talk about it. I want to see it. Stop talking the talk and get the work done."

Now this person had no idea that I hadn't even touched the surface of what I'd like to consider to be published work. I had spent more than enough time scrolling through social media, feeling like such a failure as I watched all my peers attain success, travel the world, and maintain these perfect bodies. I wondered, *Why have I been talking about this book being published for over a year but I am finding it so hard to motivate myself into writing it?*

Well, to my friend who aggressively reminded me that I simply was just talking the talk, I am sure that plenty of us could relate. A lot of the time we could just be talking the talk and not even realize it. Mentioning all these, I would like to informally thank you because now I have officially embarked on this journey, on this dream I had wanted for so long. You were truly that little push that I needed. I'm not going to be hard on myself; I know I am not alone when I do things like talk the talk, and I have heard so many others doing this before and am never really able to witness some of the things they said they would be doing. This is the reason why I decided that touching this subject is important. What I'm trying to say is something we all know: actions speak louder than our big-ass mouths. Let's stop talking about it and start being about it.

It truly always lies within just simply taking the first step.

Practicing Self-Love

There are so many ways we show that we care about ourselves. We go to the gym when we care about our physical appearance, and we eat healthier in order to speed up the process of seeing the results reflecting in the mirror. When we are going to the gym in order to improve our appearance, are we truly doing this for ourselves or to impress others by how sexy we look? Some are motivated by going to the gym because it makes them feel good—this is an act of self-love. Wanting to look better for the reaction you get when you look in the mirror—that is practicing self-love. There are thousands of ways we could show ourselves that we do, in fact, contain self-love. Throughout the years, people have been known to scold a person for being selfish—they're pretty much telling you that you are caring about yourself too much. There have been a few times in my life where I have heard the quote "The key to failure is pleasing everyone else," and for years, I had taken this quote so personally and so negatively. What I had failed to recognize was the validity behind this quote; there isn't a quote that I could agree with more.

Back to the subject of pleasing people—this was me and partially is still me. My greatest downfall has been to make sure everyone around me has been fed while my food grows cold. I have failed to enjoy nights out with friends because I get concerned about the person that's watching my child, wondering if they'd rather be doing something else with their time. I have wasted so much time on the needs of others and have never really practiced the term *selfish*. No one has ever called me selfish, and I used to think that was something to be proud of. This is something to be ashamed of because all this shows is that I never had enough love for myself; I never put myself first, and everyone around me noticed this. Overtime, this did nothing for me but to further bury me into this mind-set that I would never be good enough for anyone no matter how hard I tried to please them. This is true, because who would want to care, love, and do for someone who clearly doesn't love themselves? I have allowed people to take their frustrations out on me, literally a punching bag for someone, and day after day, I let that continue. This is not the behavior or actions of a person that contains any type of self-love.

Now when I say I want you to achieve self-love, I am talking about that head-over-heels honeymoon phase of love. This is where I am with myself now. I'm getting to know myself, I am making myself laugh, and I am so excited to be alone with me. The thought of all the new things I have decided to start doing for myself, the progress I have made, and the happiness I've brought to myself have given me more butterflies than any other person ever has. I've brought tears of joy and happiness to my own eyes because I truly and deeply love myself. I am finally at a point in my life where I can console myself, I can vent to myself, and I can hug and talk back to myself. Years ago, had someone told me I'd be this crazy over myself, for sure I'd think I would be displaying some level of psychosis disorder. No, I am gaining this level of mental-health happiness that I have never attained before. Remember, Rome wasn't built in a day, and I don't believe in love at first sight. If you've never truly loved yourself before, this is a buildup just like any other relationship.

Starting a new relationship with anyone can be scary, and there are things about the other person that you must start to question like "Do I love this person enough to deal with the way they chew?" I used this example because this might be a make-or-break for any relationship I get into—you seriously must chew like a human and not a Neanderthal. However, I am speaking from a biased standpoint, as if it were someone I'm simply dating and not in love with. That's the difference: when you're truly in love with a person, they *could* chew like a Neanderthal and it wouldn't necessarily throw you off the edge. I would simply place my hand out and ask you to spit the damn gum in my hand, immediately followed by a cute little peck on the lips.

Check on yourself the way you do with your friends, literally sit down and do a mental check. Ask yourself how you're feeling and what some alternative ways to increase that mood of yours are. I know it shouldn't have to be something to stop and think of, but I know for me, a lot of times, I do tend to get way too much into my head and my thoughts are constantly flowing. I must remind myself to stop and really pay attention to what I am doing, what I'm feeling, and what I need in order to get to where I want to feel.

I have only just recently started imagining myself standing outside of my body. I view myself as a friend that I truly cherish and care for. I hug her, I brush the hair out of her face, and I wipe the tears from her soft, beautiful cheeks. I kiss her forehead and remind her how amazing she seriously is. I remind her how many amazing people she is surrounded by and how many people see her reaching her full potential. I tell her I love her unconditionally. How corny does this sound? Extra corny to a person who's not aware of what it's like to really love themselves. Get there. It will be the most important step you'll ever take towards heading in the direction of a wonderful life.

Affirmations

Affirmation: this must be on the list of top ten favorite words or actions of mine. Learn how to do this and live by it. This goes into the subject of watching what we say; they fall hand in hand, except instead of saying less negative shit, we are focused on all the wonderful positive things we could be saying. Speaking it into existence is an amazing magic trick I've learned. Affirmations are just that, but I'd like to think of the difference in that we are speaking these positive attributes to ourselves. This is one sure way to display self-love. Wake up in the morning, turn to a mirror, and remind yourself every single day how great you are. Remind yourself how beautiful or handsome you are and whatever you want others to think and feel about you. No one will see in you what you don't see in yourself. It may make some people more attracted to your energy, your vibes, and your light.

On the other hand, it may also make those who aren't comfortable with themselves uncomfortable to see someone reaching that level of self-love. That's okay. Encourage anyone you think may need to sprinkle a little more self-love to themselves. We've been taking the back burner in our own lives for too long. Send yourself those simple reminders about your amazing self. You know more than anyone the great attributes that lie within. Also, it is very important to affirm things you want to happen in your life—affirm the dream job you want, affirm the dream car, or affirm that hefty bank account. It doesn't happen overnight, but keep believing in it.

I've been one to ignore all the signs for years. I'd go to the store and see all these decal quotes to hang up in the room—"Don't stop believing" and things of that nature—and I'd walk right past them. Today, I see things like these and think to myself, *What a perfect reminder I could be waking up to every day*. These things are not just decorations; they could act as daily reminders. These are extremely helpful. Write your affirmations out on a paper—do it every day if you have to. I wrote a list of things I'd like to affirm for my life, and I keep it in my car and read and believe and imagine them daily before I drive off to start my day. I'd affirm a job that I love, a car that I can rely on, a good credit score, and good health for me and my loved ones. Things like these were and still are important to me. One by one, these things happened for me. I encourage you all to try this. Practice affirmations and believe in good things for your life.

Blocked

We give so many people access to our lives, some we know and some we don't. This access makes us feel and act as though we do know certain people because, hey, "I just liked your picture yesterday," "I saw you were at the boardwalk," or "I know that you love to go skiing." Those who we no longer care to have in our lives continue to get this access to us—this access that allows a person to feel as if they know your progress, setbacks, and every move. In a sense, they do. We have got to stop allowing these negative-ass energies have access to our lives. No, you can't check up on me and look at my body-progress pictures. I fucking know I look good. Your loss.

We allow people to message us so conveniently to catcall us so silently. We allow everyone in and no one out. The girl that is now talking to your ex and wants to see who she's in imaginative competition with—access. The dude whom you hit it with four months ago and has yet to hit you up to see if you're breathing—access. What about that creepy-ass motherfucker that saw you at the coffee shop and followed you because your name was unique? Access.

Once I started realizing how handy the Block button could be and how refreshing it could truly make me feel, I started abusing that bitch. You will not be able to access me. Your intentions for me, my life, my goals, and my family must be great. You must be happy to be a part of my life to have access. Ever since social media has created this Block button, it has become so much easier to block people in real life. Once you remove the access to your life from someone who no longer is worthy, you start to learn that this can be a reality. These people do not need or deserve to know you; they do not deserve to hear about your accomplishments and achievements. There is no need for envy, jealousy, and anger towards you in your life when it can simply be blocked.

There are so many positive, bubbly people who truly mean it. Yes! You are from my community, and you're achieving all this wonderful shit. Go, you! Where do I sign up for this kind of people? Allow all the access to this kind of people because they are happy with themselves. They see a winner as simply a fucking winner. They applaud you, and they become inspired by you.

Break the Cycle

There are a few things that I have learned to be important in maintaining relationships throughout our lives, not just romantic relationships but friendships and family relationships as well. Of those things, I am going to list them, and for now, I'd like to specifically touch base as to why these things are important in the perspective of a parent.

There is one thing I am just recently learning. I'm raising a child, and this is a new transition in my life. There are things that I have been learning daily, and there are things that I learned within the first year of her life. I am a parent—that is a fact. There isn't a soul who can disagree with that, but there are plenty of people who can argue and disagree on the whether I am a *good* parent. Personally, I do feel as though I am a good parent; however, I am not perfect, and I am still learning every single day. Let's take a deeper look at what we'd like to consider the things that make anyone a good parent:

1. We are attentive.

    The responsibility of any parent is to keep their child safe, fed, and warm. These are the essentials. We should never let our children go without any of these necessities. Now this step alone would not be enough to consider anyone a good parent. We are good parents when we are paying attention to our children's internal needs. Are we asking our children what they are feeling and if what they feel might help them to improve what they are feeling? Are we asking our children what their greatest desires are, and do we pay attention to the signs that are unspoken? Just be there for them, through their happiest moments, saddest moments, and their most exciting times. I can only hope that my child welcomes me to her school dance so I can bust a move in the middle of the dance floor too. Just kidding! (Sort of.)

2. We practice self-care.

Yes! We are caring for ourselves. This is an important aspect to parenting. We need to focus on ourselves—not above our children and their needs but equal to. We are just as important to the quality of their lives as they are. Without us being whole, without us being mentally okay, our children suffer. It is crucial for us to pay attention to not only our physical health, in order to live a long and illness-free life to our best potential, but to our mental health as well. Sometimes we tend to forget how important our mental health can be to raise children, live a fulfilling life, and just to be generally happy. We all go through shit. This is the truth. My questions are, How have we taken that shit, and what have we done with them in our minds? A lot of us allow that shit to marinate in our minds, creating bigger piles of shit that outwardly come off as anxiety, depression, anger, and alcohol and substance dependency. If you have experienced any type of trauma in your life that you feel could have even the slightest effect on the way you behave, please sit with it and figure it out. Do not try to harbor these emotions. Do not try to stick it out. We experience pain, and just like a major knee injury by a superstar athlete, we need to work on that wound until the pain can no longer be felt.

I'd like to give you this piece of advice: Care for yourself so that your child does not pick up the energy you give off or the actions you perform in their presence. Whatever it's going to take, please never carry guilt for caring for yourself, especially if your deepest intentions are to raise an amazing, successful, happy, and heathy child. It starts with you! Guys, even if you are not a parent, this piece is so important: Take care of yourself. You will see this line a lot.

3. We listen.

I know. This sounds like number 1, but it's a little different. As far as I could remember, we have always been taught to ignore, ignore, ignore. Don't pay any mind to that tantrum this child is continuously having. Don't pay any mind to the negative behaviors that could just possibly be a cry for attention—we are encouraged to ignore all these things because, eventually, the behaviors decrease. I can agree; we are decreasing behaviors by ignoring. What we must consider is whether that is what we really find to be effective for our child's mental health in the present moment and, more importantly, for the future. Every behavior we display serves a specific function, and sometimes, the behaviors could be to get away from whatever is expected of the child. Sometimes it's to gain a specific desire, and other times, your child could just simply want the attention. I'm not encouraging anyone to allow your children to act like a damn fool in the middle of Walmart. I'm not encouraging people to give and give and give until your child grows up with a silver spoon sticking out of their ass. Please do not take my advice as if I am trying to sound like I know it all. You are going to raise your children the way you'd like to raise them. I encourage that. As previously mentioned, I am just sharing with everyone the things I have learned along the way, not only in raising my own child but in witnessing others raise theirs. Pay attention to the signs that your child has a need for; we are responsible for fulfilling them if they are our children. As parents, we are the number 1 person or people they will come to when something is just not right. Let us listen and compromise as best we can. Imagine us as adults feeling so irritated, so frustrated, and just so damn upset, and the people we look up to and love the most feel it is most effective to ignore us. These little humans feel just as strongly as we do, and let us not forget they are new to this. We need to help them through their feelings and be their emotional coaches.

Kindness

There have been so many instances in my life where people have randomly spread an act of kindness into my day. I am not sure where or who those people were, but the difference they made in that moment will be a type of feeling I could never forget and can't help but want to spread to others too. People sometimes just need that little random act of kindness to brighten their day or help move them along, and sometimes it could go further than you think. In a world full of tragedy and sadness, we can equally create kindness and love. There is one moment I will never forget, and this may in turn be of no significance for anyone else, but for me, it meant a great deal. To the woman from the grocery store, wherever you are, thank you!

I was with my young daughter, and we were gathering a few basic needs for the house. Now I won't be ashamed of the fact that money hasn't always been readily available, as there are bills and priorities. Roaming through the aisles and picking up things like milk and eggs, my daughter came across the toy aisle. She begged and pleaded with me to please get her a toy. I agreed, and I told her, "A small toy will be fine today." Excited, she picked out the perfect toy of the moment, something I knew she had her eyes set on before I had even agreed with her. Now this was a small toy, like I had requested, so I did not imagine this would cost more than five dollars. As I picked up the last few food items I needed, she sat in the back of the cart staring in amazement at this new toy. Excitement filled her thinking of the moment I could open it for her.

When we approached the self-checkout register, I began to ring out my items one by one, anxious of the end total. I finally got to her toy, and she handed it to me hesitantly, afraid she wouldn't get it back. To my surprise, the toy rang up at $12.99. I was shocked, and most of all, I could not afford to purchase this small, expensive toy at that very moment.

I regretfully informed my child I would not be able to purchase the toy for her now because it was too expensive. Tears immediately streamed down her chunky cheeks, and her pouty lips pouted even more. My heart felt for her. I got her excited, I told her yes, and here she was being told she could no longer get what she thought she was getting. What a terrible moment in a toddler's life! As I walked towards her to take the toy away from her deathly grasp, a woman from the register beside me walked over and handed me fifteen dollars. "Please, get her the toy," she said with so much kindness and empathy.

I normally wouldn't be one to take money from anyone. I never had to ask for money, and I certainly hated the idea of people in public assuming I needed the assistance. This woman had a child herself, and I knew she just simply understood and needed to forward this act of kindness. I accepted the cash because I remembered all the times I had simply needed to act on kindness. I remembered dropping off a tin can full of cash and change to a line of elementary students waiting at an ice cream truck, just imagining the one family that legit couldn't spare the extra dollar. I remembered the old man at the diner minding his business as I gave the waitress an extra twenty dollars for his meal. These acts of kindness have attracted others to do the same for me, and it truly is a beautiful thing. I can only hope and pray that everyone finds it in their hearts to randomly act on kindness. The toy that woman bought for my daughter that day spared my daughter a sad evening and, more importantly, brought a smile on all our faces.

Uncontrollable

Too many times, we find ourselves trying to control people. It may not come off this way, and we may not even realize it. It may not come in an aggressive form, but we are for sure trying to control others. It is an act of love, and it is our way of teaching them how to be in order to bring us satisfaction. In some ways, we may be trying to show these people how to treat us. Time after time, we aren't being treated the way we'd hope by certain individuals, and we need this to change. We try to control, informing this person this is how we'd like to be treated and this is what you should do. "These are the ways I want you to show me that you care." People mistreat themselves, and we try to control this. We say "This person is no good for you," "Leave them," "This drinking issue you have will end you, please stop," or "You should be seeking more from life, get educated."

There are millions of ways we try to control those around us. It's innocent and harmless, and certainly most of the time, it's because we care. We see it as a thing that needs to be done; otherwise, we do not truly care about these individuals. Some of us literally beat ourselves up trying to change people we care about, and it's like beating a dead horse. People are uncontrollable. We can never make a person feel what they do not feel or make them want to do what they do not want to do. A person may drag out an emotion and seemingly feel what you want them to feel, but this person is the only one who can decide what they want to do and what they want to feel.

As a child, I remember being told what was right and what was wrong, what I should and should not do. All these things went in one ear and out the other. I could never learn actual life lessons by simply hearing the words and information from others who have gone through it. The real lesson and experience come from having to go through these things. We are blinding ourselves trying to open the eyes of others. We are all on our own paths, own journeys, and own lesson plans. No matter how close you seem to someone in life, no matter what partnership you have, this life is yours.

Be there for people, support them, give them advice, but please stop expecting to be able to force someone to feel and do what they do not. The only thing we are in control of is the person you see when you look in the mirror. Be an example for those you love instead of trying to be a coach.

Never Second-Guess It

When we have worked devotedly to filling ourselves up and when we are overflowing with confidence and assurance of who we are, we should *never* second-guess it. When we walk through life with such boldness, others could never distrust we know our worth. Once we have reached this point, we should never let anyone else second-guess it. Our souls walk hand in hand with our bodies, loving every inch of it, striking out any entity attempting to experience it without full exceptional motive. Our souls move our legs to the rhythm of life. Entirely mindful of its surrounding and those with desires to join in, we are wise and quick—only those on our vibrational equivalence invite to dance with us.

Pressure yourself to create this energetic barrier around you, a barrier only those on your level or higher could get through. Discontinue the allowance of others in your life who treat you as a duplicated mind. Find those who seek and demand more from you because they know it is only there they will find this gratifying mentality. Never second-guess it.

Resilience

You Are Resilient

Only recently have I been told that I am resilient, and it's only been a few times. Each of the single few times I have heard this, I am instantly consumed with butterflies in my stomach. Within the flash of those couple of seconds it takes someone to let me know they feel as though I am resilient, thoughts and memories and reminders all fly across the front of my mind. I have been told I am beautiful hundreds of times—what a wonderful compliment to receive, and yet despite the numerous number of times I've heard it, it's something I still have a hard time finding to be completely true of myself. I have heard that I am smart—okay, I do like to think I am smart in some ways but am still not so sure if that's completely true either.

Resilient—that word swirls through my body, glides through my heart, and tickles my stomach. Resilient I am. That is one compliment I love to hear from those who know me very well. I have not dealt with the worst of things, but I have dealt with things that have brought me immense pain. I've mourned the loss of people still walking this earth, and I have resiliently gathered my pieces one by one and arranged them in a different way. I have earned even some extra parts of myself after the falling apart—stronger parts, smarter parts, parts that were more self-loving and nurturing. Wow! Fuck yes, I am resilient! (Exclamation fucking point!)

Let us look at the definition of *resilient*: "able to withstand or recover quickly from difficult situations." They might as well put my picture right beside this because this is one characteristic I will own.

One thing that truly has helped me become resilient is to constantly remind myself that everyone has their own struggles. When I am hurt by someone, I am reminded that the person that hurt me is clearly going through or has gone through some sort of experience in their life. I remain confident in myself and my intentions and become fully aware that I should not take such actions so personally.

Another important thing to remember when dealing with a difficult time in our lives is to remember that time heals most of our pain. Again, I am referring to caring for ourselves and breaking the cycle. Remember, even though time heals our pain, it does not necessarily heal our wounds. We still bear that memory, and the more we think about it or sometimes subconsciously carry the wound, the more it is just too deep to recover from on our own. This is where things such as disorders come through— things like anxiety, depression, and anger. This is when we need to take responsibility for our actions. We need to understand that we are, in fact, only human. We can only endure so much pain before we start to outwardly enact in behaviors deemed unacceptable by others.

I'd like to make it clear: I have been hurt by people. Most likely those who have hurt me have been hurt themselves, and it becomes a never-ending cycle—hurt people hurt people. As fate may have it, I have also hurt people. Just as I strongly believe it was never in the intention of others to hurt me, it was never the intention of mine to hurt people.

We deal with shit, and whether we'd like to believe it, we become a product of our past and a product of our pain. There are methods, ways, and techniques to overcome and face those pains. We need to do this before we become responsible for another person's heart (our partners') or another person's life (our children's). Be kind to yourself; be gentle with others. Life is beautiful, but we all struggle. Break the cycle.

I Have Anxiety

I'd like to think of myself as a professional anxiety sufferer. I do not want to claim this or confirm it; it is just what I have been dealing with, and for me to try to help others in dealing with it, I must have had some sort of experience.

I was seven years old, and anxiety had a whole entire grasp on me. At age seven, I was surrendering myself to the feeling of being anxious. I remember dropping to my knees in the middle of my kitchen one night, all alone and sobbing uncontrollably. Of course, I did not know why I was that way, why I couldn't control my emotions, or why I lived and fed off the thought of fear and worry. I just could not shake the feeling, and until this day, I am still experiencing moments of anxiousness.

There were periods throughout my life when the anxiety hibernated. I forgot I even had it, but those moments only lasted a month or so. I never really tried anything to help deal with it, and I never even thought there were ways to deal with it. I figured this is just the result of a kind, caring soul just worrying too much about the things I love. This is just who I am and the way that I am. Let's remember, we are what we think we are. The more I told myself "This is who I am," the more it became exactly who I was—an anxious worrier who could never quite get ahold of her emotions when the worry reached its peak. Maybe there were some things I had experienced as a child that possibly could have made my anxiety worse, and maybe there were actions I started to take that were reinforcing my anxiousness. I would especially become anxious about my mother, her life, and her safety. Whenever she was out, I would call and call and call until my cordless landline died and I had no choice but to wait until she walked into the door. Every time I dialed her number, and every time I reached her voicemail, my level of anxiety would increase immensely. I was reinforcing this feeling.

Within these last few years, I have tried so hard to wrap myself with knowledge and understanding of anxiety. I am no psychotherapist, but I am seeing one. I am no doctor, but I have seen many. I am not a professional, but I'd like to think, someday soon, I will be and that I will, in fact, help others overcome this increasing epidemic that so many people are suffering from.

I would just like to add here that for anyone who does not suffer from anxiety or has no idea what it feels like, please stop passing judgment. Someone has told me that I use my generalized anxiety as an excuse. If someone you love and care for tells you they are suffering from anxiety, please do not bypass that shit. It's nothing compared to a simple headache; we can't always just make the pain go away with Motrin. That shit is real, and it is debilitating in some ways. Do you think you could focus or achieve anything with a tiger staring you in the face? I think the fuck not. It obviously isn't real, and when we experience anxiety, we know there is no real tiger in front of us; however, our brains certainly do not let us shake that same exact feeling. Like I said before, for people with anxiety, you are not alone!

Here are some things I've learned about anxiety, some important things I've learned and realized that have really started helping me. Hopefully they will help you too:

1. Worry vs. trouble.

One of the things we need to focus on more while experiencing anxiety is being able to identify the difference between worry and trouble. Just because we are feeling fear does not mean we are in trouble. Sometimes when we suffer from anxiety, our minds can play tricks on us. For me, when I experience anxiety for absolutely no reason at all, I start to imagine worst-case scenarios. These thoughts make me feel as though I truly am in trouble, which, in the long run, ends up heightening my anxiety. When we begin to experience anxiety, we need to sit and start to wonder if there are actual dangers around us or any legitimate reason we may be feeling anxious. If there isn't any danger or trouble, we can then rationalize with our minds and come to terms that this is just a feeling and there are no real threats to our lives in that moment. This has helped me in some cases.

2. Cliché breathing.

    Anyone who has suffered from anxiety or felt anxious has heard this plenty of times before. Yes, you need to focus on your breathing. Whether or not you believe in meditating or yoga or any of those natural mental-healing techniques, breathing techniques are the one sure thing that is proven to help with reducing anxiety. The specific way I suggest doing this would be to take a few minutes to get comfortable where you are. Recognize the placement of your limbs—your arms, legs, head, and what have you. Pay attention to the things you are wearing—earrings, perfume, cologne, clothes, etc. Imagine how they feel and smell on you. Pay attention to any sounds going on around you, even if it's just the sound of the air vents. Once you become aware of your surroundings, you are already bringing your focus away from the feeling of anxiety.

    Next, you should close your eyes and bring your attention to the way you are breathing. Try to breathe in for ten seconds slowly and steadily. You really want to use up that complete time to inhale. I find it helpful to imagine myself inhaling a certain color that makes me feel a specific way, maybe my favorite color. Repeat this step for the entire exhale, and this time, imagine a color that you aren't too fond of being exhaled through your nose. Repeat this step until you're feeling like you could function again.

3. Social media diet.

    This is not the case for many. I know that for me, social media can give me just a little heightened boost of anxiety when I'm already feeling anxious—the idea of scrolling through the lives of others and being so consumed in what is going on in everyone else's life but my own. There have been periods of my life where I did feel as though I was slightly addicted to social media, addicted to posting my every move and addicted to checking on everyone else's every move.

We can affirm that we are strong-minded and that a lot of the things we see on social media do not have a negative impact on our lives. I would believe this if I didn't know how social media truly worked. We use filters, backgrounds, locations, and tags—everything we need to give off an illusion of the life we are living to seem a certain way. Some of us are living the lives we see, but that does not, under any circumstances, signify this person is in fact happy or content within themselves. We can sit there and be envious of a person because of their body structure, their perfectly sculpted waist, and their huge fat ass, but we have no idea if this person truly worked hard for this or easily had their body reconstructed. We see them smiling in the photo, but again, this does not signify a person's true inner happiness.

Envy is a natural humanistic emotion, and until we are fully and 100 percent happy within ourselves, we will experience envy more than a few times throughout our lives. It could be the simplest thing from a person's personified relationship that just seems to be absolutely culminating. It could be their newly remodeled kitchen we are envious of. We are envious of the life we *think* these people are living. Certainly, we are spending a lot of time forgetting to be mindful or using our time wisely. Now I do like to set a limit for myself, no more than one hour a day, or I like to try to go on a social media diet altogether.

4. Surround yourself with good people.

Imagine this feeling of anxiousness and you're around these energies that just continue to fuel your anxiety. I can't count how many times I've voluntarily and involuntarily put myself in this situation. Now remember, I am not judging anyone who has been through some shit and I wholeheartedly understand that everyone is going through their own shit. When we are actively suffering from anxiety though, I'm just suggesting we be a little more mindful of our surroundings and ways to alleviate that emotion. If you have a specific person in your life that just has the power to make you giggle, make you focus your attention on things other than your anxiety, then do that.

There are some very lucky individuals who do not know what it's like to experience anxiety and they just do not understand what you're specifically going through. It isn't that these people cannot empathize with you; it is just difficult trying to get someone to understand what it feels like to be the opposite sex. You will just never know until you experience it. Please do not kill yourself trying to get them to understand it. There are other people who do. When you need to vent about anxiety, I have found it to be most effective when venting to someone who just plain gets it.

I do not have all the answers on this specific topic. Again, I am only sharing these methods and things I have found to be helpful. For anyone suffering from anxiety, this is also just a reminder: you are truly not alone. It fucking sucks. I seriously believe that no one deserves to live in constant fear and worry.

Over the years, there have been so many wonderful, amazing, and supportive people who knew just the right thing to say—not to heal me of my anxiousness but to make me think in a much healthier direction. I am going to list them in hopes they will help you too.

Things to Remind Yourself

- "What if the worst things in your life have already happened?"

    What if anything bad that was going to happen to you in your life has already been experienced? What if all the negative things you're anticipating will *never* happen? What if it all goes up from here?

- "But . . . did you die?"

    Anxiety has never killed anyone. Feeling anxious, suffering from anxiety, or just feeling alone has never killed anyone. Remember, you are going to be okay! This feeling is a release of hormones in your body, and it takes about fifteen minutes to relieve itself if you begin thinking in a more positive direction. Remind yourself that it is just a feeling, and seek out the fact that there are no real threats to your life.

- "Laugh it out."

Go on the internet, look for funny shit, and find something to laugh about until you can't breathe. This sounds almost too simple to work, but I promise you, it does.

Wear It Well

There have been so many instances where I have opened up to a person and explained to them all the things I have had to deal with in my life. I have explained how much I suffer from anxiety and feeling insecure. I exposed my pains and trauma. No matter who they were, they would respond, "You could never tell." To me that is a compliment within itself. These people were inadvertently letting me know that I was resilient and did not allow my struggles to become who I am.

It's not necessary to always try to hide what we are dealing with. It is always okay to let people know what we are feeling and what we are going through. However, it is also important to remain positive and keep a faithful approach to life. In 2013, I was diagnosed with SLE, which is an autoimmune disease a lot of people know as lupus. This disease can be debilitating and depressing, just feeling like the odds are against you in life and then finding out that your own body is also fighting against you. It's tough, and I can't like, for a while I did let it get to me. It beat me to a depressed state; it pained me and hospitalized me. For some time, I thought I had let it defeat me. I remember reading the statistics of women diagnosed with lupus, their chances of becoming pregnant, and the risks if they do— their children face the possibility of being diagnosed with autism. These thoughts consumed me every day right alongside the swelling and the pain. The more I thought, the worse I felt physically and mentally. There are so many people out there who are feeling more pain, feeling more stress, and dealing with bigger issues, but pain is pain. I have never agreed with discrediting someone's pain because others have it worse. The idea that we are in competition with each other for pain is troublesome, and this means we are forced to heal quicker than we are ready to. I absolutely do agree that we should appreciate our situation for not being as bad as it could be, but once again, pain is pain, and we should always take the necessary amount of time needed to heal from it.

It was during my journey of physical healing when I had started to understand the practice of affirming our fate. The doctors had told me, "This disease is incurable. This will be with you forever. Remember, this disease killed your grandmother." And there were all these outside sources fighting against me as if the disease wasn't enough of a battle for me. The more I posted about the lupus walks and organizations, the symptoms, the appointments, and the tests, the worse my symptoms became. I was speaking my lupus into an even greater existence than it was before I was even diagnosed. There were more symptoms, there was a need for more medication, and there was just a downward spiral of dependency on my loved ones. I had gone through a period where it was even difficult for me to continue working. I had jumped down a seriously deep rabbit hole. Granted, I understand that sometimes when we are affected with illness, no matter how much positive thinking we do, our bodies will still suffer, but I also believe that stress of the illness causes our bodies to suffer as well. Imagine how much of the pain I was feeling was caused by stress of just knowing I was diagnosed with the same disease that had killed my grandmother at the age of forty-five.

One day, I decided to post online: "I believe I will go see my rheumatologist and she will tell me there are no more traces of lupus in my bloodwork, there is no longer a need for medications, I do not have lupus." This was me affirming to myself and everyone around me, including the universe, that I no longer believed in this illness, that I no longer needed to suffer and let this disease tear me apart from the life I have so much potential in living. I decided to wear it well. I stopped telling people when I was in pain because this was affirming the disease. I no longer cared about people knowing I had the disease because, in my head, I didn't have it anyway. I stopped taking the medications and researching the symptoms, and I just altogether envisioned and fulfilled a life without lupus. The pain and symptoms did not magically disappear; I won't sell you that false dream. Slowly but surely, I started feeling great again, and my lupus went into hibernation—this is what the doctors call it. I call it mind over matter. I call it putting good health out into the universe and claiming it as yours.

This is what I started doing with all physical and mental ailments weighing me down: shut it down and wear it well. I am flattered when someone tells me they "would've never known." These are the things that are going on within me—the pains I had gone through as a teenager, the heartbreaks, the betrayal, and the many phases of me finding myself. According to others, I wear all these things well. I have decided to use these things to help others who are dealing with them, to inspire others to use them as a reason to be stronger, a reason to come out on top and show people that despite these drawbacks, they can still win.

Sadness

Fantasy of Death

When I think of the word *fantasy*, I imagine something pleasurable. I imagine something that I would like to have or do someday. There are some people out there who have found themselves coming across a point in their lives where death had become a fantasy. Commonly, death is something people fear and dread just thinking about. We all die—that is a fact; however, death is the end of our paths. It is very unfortunate that life can be both so beautiful while also being so devastating at times.

My heart goes out to anyone who is currently feeling as though their death would solve any issues within or around them. Depression is very real and very serious and, in some cases, can end fatally. I've witnessed people with some very traumatic issues in their life experience depression, and I've also witnessed people with internal issues struggle with depression. Those cases are the ones that scare me the most. The way a person could be so beautiful, so intelligent, so loved in so many ways, and have so much potential for one of the brightest futures in the community, yet they are fantasizing the end of their lives. What we see is usually only the tip of the iceberg, and what goes on beneath the surface, not many of us will understand or know unless we are told. We've all heard the phrase "Be kind—everyone has their struggles"—this is especially important because some struggles are deeper than others. You never want to be that push that throws someone over the edge.

Instead, try to be the one to pay attention to their escalation on the ledge and be the one to help them down. With the advancement in technology, it is so easy for someone to cry out loud, yet we still disregard their plea. We scroll right by as someone is posting that they are ready to die. We ignore the people who share the posts about suicidal people seeming to be content. We need to be more open, and we need to hear these people out because when someone feels as though they have lost it all, the last day of their lives is the only thing they feel will be the end of all their pain. We can pretend to understand the root of someone's pain, and we can listen with our ears, but only when we begin to feel with our hearts and hear a person out during a time they're dealing with such heavy and immense pain, only then will they start to feel like a voice—a voice for the damaged, hurt, and sad; a voice for the depressed. It is with reason and purpose. Being introduced to the simple pleasures of life again, being reminded of the love you have for them, and simply feeling important are all ways to start.

It is our job as loved ones to support, love, and assist with the healing process because we could never—and should never—forget that it is a process.

Not Okay

It's safe to assume that the moment our daughters experience their first period, we do not expect them to go out and get a job to start gaining their independence. We do not consider them an adult, yet we continue to deal with the issue of rape, molestation, and sexual assault against children. It is quite abstruse how a man, adolescent or adult, could assume it would be reasonable for him to put his hands, or any part of his grown self, on a young female. Whatever you want to call it—rape, assault, abuse, or statutory—the female is never to blame. A man knows his boundaries; he knows the age limit in which he should and should not lay his hands on a woman.

The older I get, the more I realize how common this topic has become. We need to do better as females and speak up when these things occur. We need to stop ignoring the trauma this causes and start recognizing the cycles we could be breaking by simply speaking up and stopping others from falling victim.

We hide under the smiles during family parties, trying to push aside the image of the uncle that got a little too touchy, and we excuse it because he had a few beers. We say he didn't even realize what he was doing. We fear being disregarded and shamed because we felt uncomfortable with the way someone placed their unwelcomed hands on us. We are manipulated into thinking this is what we should be allowing or we will be punished for informing others. Our bodies have been our homes from the moment we are born. Cozy, comfortable, ours. Our privacy, our bubbles—burst by someone we think we trust.

Love

Adoration

I was your favorite waste of time, your weakness—all words comparable to love. It was a comfortable suffocation when you'd get your hands on me, cutting off the circulation of whatever limb you decided to cling to. My face was like a magnet attracted to yours, and you loved to press your cheek against mine. The face hug was what you called it. I pretended to hate it and squinched my eyes with the hundreds of face kisses that followed. It never mattered where we were; there you were—inches from my personal space. I would count down the minutes I'd get away from you only to begin the countdown to the moment I'd see you again. At times I wondered if you slept at night when I'd suddenly awake and you were right there caressing my back and kissing my neck. You wanted me forever, and to me, that felt a little too long.

Somedays you'd cry, and you'd say I never reciprocated enough emotion to keep you secure. I'd tell you to stop being so sensitive, to stop thinking so much. I'd ask you to love me less. "Maybe if you had your own life, you'd worry less," I'd say. Again, you'd cry, and in the car, you'd hook around my biceps and rest your chest on the middle console. Drenching my sleeve in tears of attachment, you'd tell me how you'll never love anyone else this way. I believed you. I read your journal one night while you had finally rested into a deep sleep. You had written to me, and I assumed these were things you were too afraid to share with me in person. You were even more sensitive in writing, but you were good. You were passionate and deep.

I continued to sweep your emotions under my rug of egotistical mind games. The love you had for me was what made me want to keep you around. It worked like a weighted blanket for me; I used it when I wanted, and when I did, I felt secure and comfortable.

After some time, the need to use it and the want for that comfortability began to decline. You'd feel it, and the clinging became tighter, the tears fell harder, and the love grew deeper. All these things in which I had no idea was even possible. Though very difficult, I slowly and passively let you go. "I'm moving on with someone new" was what I had to tell you in order to completely break your heart. It was true. The pain intensified your art, your writing, and your passion. I did something good for your life. I taught you not to love so hard, I taught you to worry about yourself, and most importantly, I taught you to never get too close.

Third-Degree Heartbreak

Why does she do this thing where she just continues to be this marvelous human being? She does this to me on purpose; she brings me to my knees and makes me grovel and beg for more of her natural self. Why does she read the kind of books that she reads? Why does she sing those songs the way she do? Everything she did once harmonized my brain waves but now screeches at me like nails on a chalkboard.

I begin to wonder, *Is today even Tuesday?* I'm torturing myself, taking myself out of situations I enjoy the most, and bringing myself to the locations I know she visits often. I am sabotaging my mind wondering if I'll ever be able to be in that position again.

The wires of the intuitive connection I strongly believed we had shared are charred to an unrecoverable state. If I happen to stumble across her mind when she glances towards my favorite novelty items, I will never feel the instinct I once had before. This woman loves shopping at savers, and here I am searching through the nineties jeans being sold at ten bucks apiece. I'm beginning to think what kind of man originally owned these jeans and, more importantly, if he had third-degree heartbreak too.

Just then, I realize I'm about to ruin my entire day as I start to think about the day she held my hand, caressing each palm line trying to tell my future. "I have studied Chinese palmistry," she had joked. Part of me wishes that were true, because she would've seen our fate. She would've known I was going to break her heart entirely. Shit, I wish I had studied the damn handreading myself. I had no idea how my actions could cause self-infliction, infliction that would slowly break down my main organ to nothing but a mere vessel, pumping blood through my miserable body.

Everywhere I go I'd see faceless women, women with nothing but skin color and hair. I have no idea what a woman's face looks like anymore, other than my family members' and hers. I guess it is easier this way, since I know there will be times I will need a night of satisfaction, and it will be best if they didn't have a face.

Maybe this is my karma. I've walked very casually by sundresses drenched in tears. I've seen and heard so many women shower their souls to me, and I've responded with a simple drawback. Yes, this is my karma for sure—I'm in line here wanting to bleed out on the register table, dying to tell the woman who works here how badly I messed up. I'd like to beg her to provide me with something for this ache in my chest. Maybe another man, in his eighties now, has passed down the secret to healing a manly broken heart, and they're selling it here at the secondhand store. This is clearly a part-time job for her, and she's just trying to get through the night.

Why do they claim this person to be the one that got away, this woman that supposedly got away but never did because she's all I ever think about? There's no way she's anywhere near gone; she's there present, 110 percent envisioned in my brain, and I don't think I can rid myself of her. I realize that I can't even have a conversation with somebody without them mentioning a word she just so happened to say before without me giving off some sort of signal that I am, and always will be, thinking of her.

There may have been a night or two when I take a deep breath and fog up my glasses to clean them with my shirt, hoping I'd maybe see a nose or a pair of earrings on the faces of these women, but they would never show.

Do It Raw

Things just feel so much better when it's raw.

For once in your life, let someone tell you that you *should* do it raw. I'm not talking about sex. I've heard there's this new trend where hiding what we think and feel has become popular. This is how people respond: they respond to the unknown, and they respond when they aren't aware of what we feel. This works for those of us who are trying to attract someone that's into the idea they *think* they have of us. How much easier it is to conceal what we truly feel and who we truly are to paint this picture of this person we would love for everyone to see.

We have grown so accustomed to posting pictures that are filtered, edited, and cropped—hardly ever do we witness raw photos. This generation has so much potential to make raw happen. I have recently started attending poetry slams where people are laying it all out on the table for strangers. It is the most beautiful experience I have had the pleasure of seeing. I love when I see a person can be themselves remorsefully. Ugly, battered, broken, and bruised, "Here I am—take it or leave it." It's uplifting to know that we can be our worst version of ourselves, and yet if we are true to who we are and have faith in the future, we can absolutely find genuine people who will love us. When we are constantly trying to live in this vision of ourselves that is solely just that—a vision. We become accountable for harboring and hiding our true selves, which in turn only deteriorates our inner characters. This is when mental health becomes compromised, relationships fail, and we just begin to snowball a ton of issues. Just imagine a world where we are always our authentic selves, where we aren't focused on attracting those who are also perceiving themselves to be something they're just not. Wear vulnerability like a scarf—who gives a rat's ass what people think about it? Because the right people and those who have good intentions for you are going to love that shit, and those who don't are eventually going to find a way outside your life, exactly where they fucking belong. Vulnerability and rawness are so beautiful. It's what we need in this world. We need to feel more and think less. Do it all with more heart.

In Love with Pain

We had two bleeding hearts, and they were reaching out for each other.

We met in sadness—we fell so deeply in love with it. We bathed in it and cleansed each other in tears. Your sadness helped me through mine and mine through yours, but we were stuck.

We just could not seem to come back from it, and it grew to become our relationship.

You tugged and tugged on my shoulders, begging me to wake from misery, not knowing you helped me get comfortable here. I made this little nook in the corner of my mind, and though dark and gloomy—like a rainy, chilly day—I was so comfortable here.

I had grown accustomed to you easing the pain, and what could you ease if the pain ever left?

The comfort of cuddling through sad stories, kissing away the ache, and making love to me helped reduce the anxiety. I grew so much love for this comfortable sorrow.

We all deal with darkness one way or another. Sometimes it's relaxing—it's how we sleep.

I remember the night I didn't want you to sleep. I wanted endless love on that very night. It was as if my skin was an empty canvas—blank, pale, and white. Your lips were the brushes filled with vibrant colors of red, pink, and blue. You had one goal: cover my canvas entirely.

What good was a man if he couldn't feel my pain? I ached in ways I could not verbally express. I had developed this strong habit of harboring emotions, specifically those most painful. It was the only way I knew how to feel.

I cried to you because I wanted to accept and appreciate this love. I wanted to dance in it. Most of all, I wanted to reciprocate it. This is the type of love I had been deserving of. You made beautiful attempts to create my happiness.

With each bath, I'd cleanse. With each shower, I'd drench myself in beautiful rays of positivity while shedding the dead particles of negativity that ate at my skin the entire day. I'd breathe in and hope to grasp that ache in my chest and release it as I exhale.

The more I craved happiness, the less I craved you. I yearned for me to love me the way you had loved me.

You'd remind me daily all about the beauty that lies within me and even more about the beauty that lies on the outside.

Lies.

All I could see were your lies. I didn't see this beautiful being you just so happened to be in love with. I didn't see my soul shine from within. I couldn't see my heart glow. All I could see were your lies.

One night while you were mummifying my body, wrapping me in soft white cloth, rubbing the soreness from my bones, you told me, "No one would ever love you this way." I peered down at my damaged self and nodded in confirmation, for once some truth to your words.

I couldn't remember if you'd been educated in the medical field, but you treated my wounds so well. This one bandage I wore for years, right across the left side of my chest. It was soiled and curled over, starting to peel from my skin. The bandage was holding on for dear life, the same way my mind did. Multiple times you'd reach for it, attempting to smooth it down or peek in on it, and immediately, I'd smack your hand away. Still so sensitive, still felt so fresh, I could never let you go there. I didn't want you to ease this one. I didn't want you to see how grave it had been all these years. You would probably say I needed help, and you would think I needed immediate attention. I'd hide it for as long as I could.

It was when you were asleep when I decided to watch you beside me. I looked within the crevices of your body, marveling at your exquisite hygiene and clean skin. Your face was impeccable, flawless. Brushing my hand across your chest, I could feel something beneath your thin T-shirt. I began to lift your shirt at the line of your neck, looking below to find a bandage, a clean fresh wound above your strong beating heart. I realized we must end this now. It was in that moment I noticed the pain you were causing yourself trying to heal me from mine.

The Wish

It was your twenty-fifth birthday, and you were less than satisfied with living the life you were living. You woke up and had coffee, hoping for it to be the best cup you'd ever experience because it was on your short, simple list of things you wanted to do today. The coffee was burnt, and there were maybe two sugars less than what you had asked for. It was okay though, because maybe the girl who made your coffee was also less than satisfied with the life she had been living. Just like you. You were like this, always considering the other person even if they randomly flipped you the bird while driving on the highway. *That person is just having a bad day,* you'd say to yourself.

You wanted to go for a beautiful walk beneath the sun and the trees. "Spend time with nature" was what it read on your list. And you did. You took your walk, and you spent time with nature.

It was the third item on your wants for your wonderful twenty-fifth birthday. You wanted ice cream—black raspberry deliciousness with rainbow sprinkles on a sugar cone. When you got to the ice cream shop, they had run out of black raspberry ice cream and they had only chocolate sprinkles left. That was okay.

Fruit. You wanted a supercolorful fruit salad today. For some reason, that didn't happen.

A few other things on your list included some enjoyable stress-relieving activities like painting, drawing, and writing. You did some of this but couldn't quite find the creativity you knew you had within you.

Your day was still going just fine. You wanted your own ice cream cake, and you wanted to make the grandest of wishes. Your older cousin called your mother and invited you over to celebrate the birthday you and your cousin shared. And you get to share the cake too. Mosquito-bitten and thin, you and two others blew out the candles following the awkwardly sung "Happy Birthday" song. Your wish had a 33 percent chance of coming true. It was a not-so-memorable birthday for you, the most unmemorable birthday of all, so you would never forget it.

That night, you sat up on the second-floor porch and you cried. You thought to yourself how the cry should have been on your list. A moment to release. It was the only thing from this not-so-special day that felt so good. All you cared about were the simple things. It never failed for your head to be looking up while being out in the middle of the night. The one thing that had always made you feel good were the stars. What drew you to them? You'd never stop looking up. Just then, it happened. Just for you on this not-so-special day, a shooting star slowly made its way before your eyes. It wanted you to notice it. You quickly squeezed your eyes shut as tight as you could, and you wished. Of all the people on this earth, you were sure this was your star, your wish. A 100 percent chance it'd come true. The final thing on your wish list, the one thing you thought had the least chance of happening—*Please let him cheat on me!* you thought. You thought it so hard. You were in a situation so terrible that your most important wish was to be cheated on.

Your day and night had ended with this. It didn't occur to you to try to fulfill your wish list the next day because your mind didn't work that way. Once a chance had ended, there were never any other opportunities. He was bringing you a gift since he didn't get to see you yesterday. You were not thrilled really, just hoping your gift lacked the drama.

Your phone rang, and it was him; he was outside. "You need to come outside," he said. "We need to talk in the car." Terrified at what could possibly be the reason behind this, you went anxious-filled and nervous. You sat in the passenger seat, and he cried. To your surprise, he was vulnerable to you right now. Upset.

"What is it?" you asked. He could barely look at you, and you assumed it was because he was embarrassed by his tears. "I cheated on you," he confessed. You're shocked and not because you thought this was something he would never do but because wishes *do* come true. How quickly this one happened for you. You sat in silence knowing this was the beginning you've been dying for.

You brought out your best acting skills and cried and yelled. "How could you do this?" you said with a smile behind your frown. He admitted that something compelled him to. "She lured me," he assured. None of that mattered; you were free—his explanations and excuses were irrelevant. This was the beginning of something new for you; you gained freedom and happiness, but of all the things you gained from this, you gained faith—faith in what's written in the stars.

Red Flags

Very rarely have I been exposed to the discussion of red flags, and maybe I have, but I never really paid attention to it. Maybe it went right in one ear and out the other. I just feel as though it's very important to cover these bases to prevent anyone from ever being caught up in a situation anything less than harmonious.

There are so many young women with exceptional potential to be someone. I would love to do everything I can to ensure these women are not shaken out of their excellence by another person. I want to feed their minds and souls with enough confidence to get them through every day of their lives. I don't want to just get them through it; I want to help them go above what is expected, soar amongst the stars, and achieve wonderful, beautiful things.

Abusive relationships make up a huge majority of relationships starting from a very young age. Only recently have I had it brought to my attention that they are not educating young girls and boys on the consequences of enduring an abusive relationship. I want to simply include a list of red flags if this is something that could bring awareness to the well-being of any individual and assist them in creating a loving and healthy environment for any relationships they decide to be a part of.

1. Your partner attempts to control your friendships. Opposite sex or not, if you are in a relationship with someone and they feel as though they have a say in whom you choose to be friends with, especially if you are truly just friends, this is a red flag. If you decide to be friends with people, it is because they bring some sort of joy and happiness into your life at some point. Another person should never try to decrease that level of joy for you in any way. A

loving, healthy relationship will involve always wanting the best for you.

2. Your partner displays a grave level of insecurities. This is the start of a very bad situation. Misery loves company, and when someone isn't happy with themselves, they will try to bring others down with them or accuse and be suspicious of every event going on around them.

3. Your partner is protective over the way you dress. Any secure person is not going to allow the way you dress to be an issue.

4. The way this person treats others they care for. Pay attention to how their loved ones view them. Listen beyond words on things that are said about them.

5. You need to share your personal information. When a partner doesn't feel safe allowing you to keep your personal information such as passwords to yourself, this is a red flag. This is a person that feels as though you are not entitled to your individuality; they do not trust you, and they could become worse.

6. You feel as though you're constantly being watched while out in public. Your partner is focused on your actions and your words when around others. You have to walk on eggshells wherever you go and whoever you're with.

These are just a few important warning signs that come along with some form of domestic violence. This does not mean if your partner shows one of these signs, they are destined to be a violent partner; however, these are things to pay attention to. It is easy to become accustomed to a relationship that requires all these things and see nothing wrong with it, especially if both parties agree that each should have access to their partner's privacy. Over time, it does become mandatory and the couples see this as necessary—that's their choice. When you feel it is a forced topic, speak up. You are entitled to be your own person and have your independence.

Mermaid
The Girl Who Sacrificed Her Soul

She got her legs, and she got her man. This was the life she had fought for, so how could she possibly want or need anything more? After riding on their boat off into the sunset, the mermaid and her prince had planned to spend the rest of their living days together happily—the way all fairy tales ended. Except in this one, happy only lasted so long.

As the years passed, happy was reduced to contentment. Contentment turned to comfortability, and after a while, the prince became just an average man who had been with a woman for way too long.

This man had an all-inclusive deal, a "main course, beverage, and dessert" deal that would more than satisfy any man, and still he would keep the menu folded in his back pocket. Sitting across from him, lost deeply in his eyes while caressing his larger-than-normal fingers, she reminded him again, "I don't think I could ever love another man this way." She smiled. "I'm crazy about you, babe." Little did she know that as she poured herself out to him. His glass of confidence was overflowing. There was never much of an equal mutual response; most times it was just a meager "I love you too"—empty and meaningless. To her, this time alone together meant he was here in this moment with her and no one else. She didn't have to check social media to see where he might be or whom he might be with. Here was where he was because, of course, it was where he wanted to be, right? She would reassure herself a thousand times a day, "He's with me because this is what he wants." There was always this inner disagreement she would have with herself about what he really wanted. On most days, she would blame herself for his distant mannerisms, and other days, she would blame his true feelings. All his hurtful actions were justifiable, and there would always be something that she could do differently to prevent those things from happening.

On the days she truly believed she wasn't doing enough, she would find ways to do more. *Maybe he would love a new pair of diamond earrings and a gold bracelet to match. Maybe I could serenade him with old-school R & B while dressed in an overly expensive lingerie set,* she thought. In almost all these instances, there would be a blank stare on his face, full of dissatisfaction, but still, she tried.

It was on a late Sunday afternoon in the kitchen when her stomach flipped. It turned and tightened, unsettling and setting off the anxiety triggers in her brain. *Something isn't right.* She waited for the anxiety to settle and reassured herself she was being her normal, overthinking self. But the flip happened again, more intense, and this time with an intuitive vision. It was him she saw, with women—women she had never seen before. They were educated and fashionable—a few qualities she knew she was lacking. He looked the way he had when he first met her, interested. They're laughing and enjoying a simple time together, just as she and Eric used to do. Suddenly, the vision was gone, and he walked in.

"I'm going to take the time out today to go for a jog," he informed her. Pressing her face to form some sort of grin, she nodded, and as she watched him head out, skepticism rolled through her like loud thunder at 3:00 a.m. in August.

A sudden realization came over her, and all she could think about was how she threw all her fucking eggs into his shitty-ass basket. She really gave him her all, and he could give two shits less, just here for show. She was in love with a man that kept a stone face with every kiss she laid on him. All these thoughts of his recent behaviors flashed through her mind, and all she felt was grief; she knew she was losing him.

After all the things she had been through with him, she couldn't let him go. Some of the best days of her life began and ended with him. He was everything to her. Everything. She would allow him to break her heart a thousand times before she'd walk away. Willing to experience pain time and time again from him, she stayed. She pushed all her thoughts, worries, and intuitive visons to the very back of her mind. She stayed. Of course, her friends talked their shit, and some of them even walked away. Why would they want to remain friends with someone who allowed that negativity in her life?

Little by little, everything she had outside of him began to fade. In the end, she was left with him and him only. With every conversation they had, his annoyance grew and tolerance decreased. How could he continue to want to be in a relationship with her when he had just plain grown apart from her? The more she gravitated towards him, the more he pulled away. They say opposites attract, and once upon a time, they were opposite and the attraction was real. The more she tried to be part of his life—a part of his interests, pleased in doing what it was he wanted to do—the more the opposition turned, and she became more and more like him. She was no longer her own person, and he was no longer in love. She made him her whole cake when he should've only been a slice.

He lost the girl he fell in love with, and she lost herself.

Healing

There aren't too many ways to describe a broken heart, and I'm speaking specifically for myself. Maybe other talented people could come up with all the synonyms, analogies, and words to explain what it feels like to experience heartbreak. For me, it was just a feeling, a feeling that would not go away. It slept with me, it ate with me the occasional times I had grown an appetite, and it even created art with me. I had a specific time of day where I would allow myself to release the cries that had filled me like breastmilk. The more I'd let it produce, the more it hurt, and sometimes when I'd release it, I'd feel a sense of relief in some ways, until the next day, when it would start to fill again. Some days I wasn't sure I could ever get through it. I was grieving. Someone had taken all that I was and deemed it not good enough—not good enough for them when I had tried to conform the best ways I knew how. Memories of us laughing and being friends stormed through my mind, and I was angry. All I could do was be angry and sad. I did not understand it nor did I care to try to. I thought this was so cruel, and I would never survive from it. I cried, and I begged for this person to reconsider, for him to imagine all the ways I could adapt and become what he needed. Each time he denied me, the pain was reinforced. I was reopening the wound each day.

I'm not sure why or how, but I stopped setting aside that time to cry. I told myself, "I can get through this." That was the first step to healing and believing that I could. I spent months before this telling myself "You are *not* going to be okay. This is *not* okay." I had lived in that thought and tortured myself by simply just believing that I could not grasp life. The moment I started thinking about the possibility of this pain healing, it started to become more and more attainable. Instead of writing letters to him in my journal, I started writing letters to myself. Instead of imagining a successful future with him, I started imagining a successful future for myself. Little by little, day by day, I took the love I had for him and showered it on myself. At first it was a little bit of love here and there, and gradually it grew until one day, I was soaked in love. Love for myself. So much love for myself I didn't even know what to do with it. So much love for myself it started to outwardly show. It showed in the way I acted, in the way I looked, and in the way I began to treat others.

The process of healing is just that, a process. There are no deadlines or rules. You simply heal, one step at a time, taking as much time as you need. Never let anyone try to rush your pain away.

Inspirational

What Sets You Apart?

There are people that I have the privilege of knowing, and these people are truly inspiring to me. I have seen people suffer from the most severe cases of anxiety, insecurities, being hurt, and just being a huge codependent of those they love. These are all the fundamentals people can use as an excuse to settle in their lives.

One person had dealt with all these things in her short young life and yet has had the ability to dust herself off and create the life she *deserves* to live. At one point, this girl did not feel comfortable in her own skin, though she was always beautiful to me. She did not have her dream job, and her love life was a roller coaster. This woman was the go-to support system for everyone around but had very little time to support herself—pouring herself into everyone's bowl, practically emptying herself. She wore it so well. Her presence, regardless of her pain, never failed to bring a smile on my face.

Over the years I had watched her, and I have been so very lucky to be able to witness one of the most amazing life-changing realizations—this woman started to faithfully work daily on her physical health, pushing her body to limits she didn't even know were possible. Every day there was a new goal and a new limit. She reached up and sought education in order to attain her dream job, which she now has. This woman placed herself first and showed the world that it is okay to wake up one day and decide that *you* are going to change this life, decide that *you* are done feeling anything less than spectacular.

Her life now truly gives me the chills; she inspires me and motivates me. The moral and point of the story being, What sets you apart? What makes this woman and her struggles different from all of us and different from us deciding this same exact thing? What stops you from going out and getting the life you truly deserve? It is so much easier to make excuses for ourselves than to get up and do what we need to do in order to obtain the life we want to live. It is so much easier to continue down the path we have been treading on for so long. Easier never leads to a fulfilling path. Ask yourself, What sets you apart?

Be the Voice

Fear holds so many people back from many things in this life, sometimes from some of the most important things they could ever do. There have been so many instances in my life where I had allowed fear to take over my ability to accomplish things or do something I truly wanted. There have been people in my life that have persistently been *the* voice I needed to help me with that little push. In a lot of those cases, I'm sure those people had no idea how much they truly did help me by simply reassuring me I could do it or by speaking up for me in times of need, just having my back in certain situations. Once I realized how far those voices had pushed me, it really encouraged me to be the voice for others, even if they were total strangers. There is one instance that has really continued to encourage me to do so, and it happened like this:

During my time in college, I had taken classes all around the campus. Some of those classes were in a stagelike setting, and others were just in small classrooms. I had met people, befriended people, and been introduced to diversity. One class I had was in a very small class setting. It was a math class, and I must add how much I hate math. Math is literally the worst subject to me ever. There really is no reason for me to add that fun fact.

Anyway, on the first day of class, some students were on time, and others not so much; maybe even a few students felt as though they didn't really need to show up to read the syllabus. I felt it had been very necessary at the time to stop by the vending machine to fuel up on some snacks for the three-hour class that awaited me. I remember arriving to the class and there were quite a few available seats. I had always been one to sit in the back corner of every class if that seat was available. Lucky me, plenty were available in that class. I took my seat and quickly began to open the wrapper of my granola bar, because no one likes hearing all that noise while the professor introduces themselves. While waiting for the professor to even arrive, I had taken observation of my surroundings, per usual. Here are the things I had noticed: (1) The one individual with the shiny green hair—I feel like there was always at least one of those unique individuals in my class. If this is you and your hair, you are unique and amazing, and I thank you for being brave enough to be you. (2) The guy who carried all their books in one backpack even if it was just that one class he had that day. (3) The last thing I noticed had been the small table aligned with the desks. I didn't think too deeply into this, shockingly, but it was certainly something I had noticed.

The icebreaker is what they call it when the professor starts to make us all go around the classroom and introduce ourselves, our majors, and why we wanted to take the course. Nine times out of ten, we are there because it's a requirement. I've yet to meet a handful of people who love math.

It had been about fifteen minutes into the class, and I couldn't help but notice a heavyset girl standing in the doorway, seemingly bashful. I might have looked over in her direction about three times before she made her way out into the halls, not to be seen again for the remainder of the class. I wondered what she was doing, then it occurred to me: she may have needed the table, but the only available seat to go with it was directly beside the professor. I imagined she had arrived late and was embarrassed to go up in front of the class to grab that seat. I imagined she might have been ashamed to even have to use an accommodating seating arrangement. Sadness filled me, and I wanted to chase her down the halls and tell her it was okay, tell her I'd be happy to grab the seat for her. I just knew it was too late. I reminded myself to do all I could next class to make sure this girl did not have to feel like missing an entire class was a better option than feeling embarrassed.

The next time we met for class, it had been five minutes into the class and I noticed she still was not there, and there was the table lonely and ready for her. The professor continued to teach when I felt her shadow behind me, once again standing in the doorway. I hated that I had to assume this was the reason why she was standing there, but I had nothing to lose by simply getting up and grabbing that chair for her. I placed it right near the table and hoped she would take a seat, and she did. She turned over and smiled at me, this sigh-of-relief kind of smile, and I knew she needed this more than I could have imagined. That day forward for all these classes, I arrived early and made sure that seat was exactly where she needed it to be for the rest of the semester.

We never got to know each other, and most of the time, she had no idea that I had made these attempts at ensuring she wouldn't miss any more classes. It was very rewarding for me to know that I was in the smallest way helping her because everyone has their struggles, and all they need is a little kindness and compassion. It was never something I did to brag about or to make myself look good; it was a situation I never mentioned until now. I just feel as though it's important for us to learn that if we can be on the lookout for people who are afraid to make their own moves or speak their own minds, it would go further than we think to do that for them.

Multidimensional

Not everyone has dimensions to their character; some people are just straight away easy to read—these people are just easy to predict, easy to figure out, and plain easy to get along with.

I am not one of those one-dimensional people.

Like an onion, there are so many layers to me, and it is not easy for me to reveal my center to most.

Complex and full of flaws, I do not consider myself to be an easy person to deal with.

I am multidimensional.

With so many directions within me, one would become deeply lost.

I take a seat at the center of this labyrinth, grasping my heart with patience.

To the one who accepts the challenge, when you find your way without exhaustion, without confusion, and with persistence, my heart is yours.

Shituations

Mixed Signals

Every shituation gives off mixed signals. You fail to recognize that any signal anyone is giving you, other than a direct indicator they are in fact interested in you and are trying to pursue you, is *not* a mixed signal. It is also a clear indicator they are *not* trying to pursue you. When someone is giving mixed signals, it's because they are feeling mixed emotions, which quite frankly means sometimes maybe they're interested in you and sometimes they're not. They got better shit to do than to see where things go with you, and the few times they try to see you is just extra time on their hands. They're bored. I hate to be this Debbie Downer; I hate to sound so pessimistic. What I'm trying to tell you is that even if this person is slightly interested in you, even if they do want to take you out and see where things go, it is not what you deserve. You do not deserve mediocre half-ass efforts. Do not settle for the person you *think* you want just to show yourself they may or may not be interested. There are just no such thing as mixed signals, because you could absolutely tell whether they want you or they don't and they're just passing time fucking with your head.

I am being so harsh and critical because we all deserve to find that kind of situation where it's not questionable. None of us deserves a shituation. We deserve the kind of experience where we aren't concerned for this person's intentions for us, because it's clear. We deserve to feel when someone truly gives a shit about us without having to hear it. What has become afflicted about feeling for someone who can't exactly reciprocate these emotions is that we lose sight of the fact that we are truly the prize here. We should never feel stricken with lust to the point that we lose sight of who we are and what we are worth. What we must bring to the table is far more admirable than this other person can usually recognize. When this is the case and when this person is literally blind to your greatness, they are not for you.

Chocolate

It has been said that chocolate is an aphrodisiac. It releases chemicals into your brain, chemicals that would give one the feeling of being in love and being full of joy. Dark chocolate contains the most benefits, including working as an antidepressant. According to theories of some psychologists, even just the smell of chocolate could help slow down brain waves, helping people feel calm. It is most commonly enjoyed as a dessert after meals to increase the sensation of satisfaction and gratification. We add it to foods that are known for increasing wellness, such as strawberries, bananas, and melons. We literally add chocolate to everything—cookies, cake, shakes, pancakes, and even alcoholic beverages. After some time though, humans create a taste aversion for the foods that make them feel anything less than well.

You know that piece of chocolate you'd binge on until it made you feel like shit? After so long, you'd try to take a break from it until, two weeks later, you're craving it again. "A little piece won't hurt," you say aloud. You treat yourself to mistreat yourself. Why do you always miss the bad stuff?

He was that annoying-ass piece of chocolate that you just couldn't stop thinking about. He was your bad habit—no good for you—and occasionally, you would still lust over the sugar high you'd get from the sweet taste of his lips. His supple brown skin against yours would feel therapeutic and soothing in ways you had searched for at the local beauty supply store, sometimes within lotions and other times in a bath salt. He had the secret ingredient you were looking for, the one that made your skin feel incredibly soft and tender. You knew that even if you looked unpleasant, he would still want so badly to squeeze the dip in your waists and pounce on you like a lion would its next prey. You would wonder how you could look in the mirror and list all your own flaws, from the prickly tiny hairs above your upper lip to the curve of your middle toe—it always leaned too far to the right—but his perspective of you still made you feel as though he saw you as this beyond-perfect human being. You developed an addiction to the feeling of feeling irresistible, and in the moment, you indulged and savored every ounce of this guilty pleasure. As he began to tenderly press his lips against your stiff neck, which is now covered in an abundance of goosebumps, your mind dived into the negative side of the pool, and you began to remember the feeling you knew would consume you the second he left.

It's gone, and just as you do with that chocolate, you take one more piece, one more bite—it won't hurt. But it always does.

Roosevelt

You found a dime stuck to the inside corner of your sock drawer, a perfect match for the quarter you remember you had in your wallet. No swipe necessary for something as miniscule as a thirty-five-cent pack of Winterfresh gum. You now have twenty-four minutes to clear the clutter from the coffee table, sweep your area rug, and dust the television in your living room. You don't even have to worry about your bedroom because tonight isn't the night you introduce your bedroom. You have that twelve-pack of unscented tea lights so you could bring a flame to a few—

Don't forget, tonight isn't the time for you to set the mood.

You remember the nightstand in your room could use a little polish, but the fresh orange-peel scent will be obvious. Your jeans hug you a little too snug; you might want to get more comfortable.

Oh man, your toes aren't freshly painted.

How about your hair? Is it soft enough to rub on? How does it smell? That floral shampoo never really lasts long; maybe you should have washed it once more, but you don't want to drip like a wet poodle.

A text comes through, your heart sinks, and you scan your private place one more time.

A door is open, the couch bed is out, and the sweatpants are easier to remove than those snug jeans would've been.

Your bedroom becomes open house, and you can't help but satisfy your desire to embrace the scent of his deodorant as you cuddle up under his arms.

There is a scent of Winterfresh on his breath—or maybe it is Spearmint.

These smells are all accompanied by an upside-down stomach—that "will I get a text tomorrow" anxiety feeling, that "did you try as hard as I did" feeling, that "did you find a dime too" feeling.

Bird Shit

At first, his name would come up so often, and it was because of me. I would bring him up all the time. I always wanted to talk about him. I always wanted to know if maybe a source of a source would leak who had been in his bed the weekend before the last—perhaps someone just happened to mention a one-night stand they had with him to their friend while using the public restroom at a bar. I would continuously be talking shit, because who would assume I still cared if all I did was run my mouth hoping a flock of birds flying south would let loose and shit on his entire car? "Is that bird shit?" he'd question. I didn't have the balls to key that shit. He had been waving clear-cut signals that he didn't want to see me anymore, and I could not help but obsess over what could have caused him to feel this way. We would have sex so often and so good there's no way he didn't enjoy it. After all, he was the one who would call me late in the evening on the weekends. I'd send a check-in text here and there to see how he was doing, only to be ignored until the next day. It was so fucking frustrating. I was pretty much in love with this guy; he was all I could think about. Weekend after weekend, I'd lay "asleep" for as long as I could, waiting on a text that never came, and I'd never really get enough rest checking in on my phone every toss I had made.

He was a real Columbian fuckboy. He really was just doing him, and it made me sick. I'd suck it up and text his dumbass anyway. Of course, on a Saturday after 1:00 a.m., when I had just seen a social media post of him leaving the club, it'd be best to catch him as soon as he was grabbing a bite from the food truck; that way, he'd come straight over to my place, and he did. The love was so aggressive, passionate, and just always so extra, like a dramatic romance scene in a novella. It'd go down like this: He would send the text that he was outside my house, and I'd open the door in a short, little boy-short type getup with a huge T-shirt over it—I loved the idea of him assuming I might be wearing another man's shirt. The next thing would be him catching a great view of my ass as I ran up the cold hallway steps. Teasing him before I get to tease him, I knew exactly what my intentions were. Some days he'd be feeling extra nice and reach over for a quick going-up-the-stairs booty grasp. I loved that shit. Closing the door behind us, we'd barely make it to my room before the huge T-shirt was removed. My guess was his first thought was in fact that it was another man's shirt—what I liked to imagine that as. I had my hair in a bun and my glasses on, playing the role of the late-night weekend studious character. I had never had anyone so gently and combatively remove a hairpiece from my hair, painlessly and with full intention of attack.

Pushing me against the wall, getting a firm hold of my neck, he kissed me like I was a whore and he was using his whole life savings on me tonight. I thought he was taking it too far when he tossed me on my bed, but it felt so damn good. I needed this, and this was the type of shit that had me constantly wanting more. How fucking annoying how good he was at this shit. He made the most satisfying love to me, like too good not to think about the whole entire next day.

Another week full of anxiousness, every text I'd get that wasn't from him. It was that type of shit I'd set myself up for. He's clear about what he felt; it's just me who needed to be clear what I felt. In the end, there was never a point to admit to what couldn't be reciprocated.

Trauma

The Good Girl

The moment someone passes away, everyone loves to imply how much of a "good" person he or she was. The person who passed could have committed thirty sins a week, and yet because they're dead and gone, they will always be remembered as a "good" person. That's bullshit, huh! Not too many people have the audacity to disrespect the dead by announcing the time Jimmy smacked the prostitute because he didn't want to pay her.

Bella was whimsical, friendly, sweet, beautiful, and beyond everything else, she was a good person. This is a stated fact.

Just because she had it never meant she had to flaunt it. And trust me, she had it all. The kind of girl you could be around, and the wisp of her almond eyes would send you into a vortex of all things beautiful. She never had to speak about the things she had done in her life to become so amazing; in fact, she didn't even realize how amazing she was herself. Her breasts were perfect in size, but she wouldn't shop for the low-cut blouse to draw attention to them. The beams of light that would radiate from her personality were comparable to the northern lights—colorful, soft, and bright. She was simply pleasurable to engage with in any form.

The story of Bella is quite interesting because, as so many believe, she ran off and sacrificed herself for her father, and then *boom*, she got trapped in a castle, and she fell in love with the monster who lived there who turns human again soon after. They lived happily ever after, blah-blah.

Wrong.

As with any on-the-surface story, we have no idea what happens beneath it, and that's okay. Here's the truth:

Bella was different, a unique individual with so much creativity just within her tiny pinky toe. With very few men to woo her in the village, she knew it would take someone just as unique as herself to sway her into romance.

There was John, the original senior fuckboy, and despite the way the original story has been told for years, this is the piece they like to omit. Bella loved John, and of course, she hated the way he was so full of himself, so arrogant, and in some ways, so ill-mannered; but behind closed doors, he adored her, and he saw her for what she truly was—a magnificent and delicate rose.

The magic within her soft small palms could bring him back down from his high horse and humble him to a socially acceptable level. John beside Bella was nothing more than himself—intelligent, caring, and kind. The man that she inspired him to be was the kind of man she could see herself with forever; unfortunately, forever never really holds up to its description.

"Why can't you always be this magnificent man that I see here before me?" she asked, running her fingers through his head of silk. "I love this person that you've become with me. I just wish everyone else could see it," she continued. Drawing herself back from his hard-exterior chest, she saw through it all and embraced his soft heart. His response was a tender, soft kiss, making it hard for her to continue prying on the subject any longer.

They would spend most of their time together behind closed doors, because that was where John made her feel like the most essential piece of his life. She would experience some of her most pleasurable moments with this version of him. Avoiding the public eye and experiencing the sensational points of love were exactly where she would always want to be. Interlocking her fingers with his, she thought about how no other man's fingers would ever fit hers so perfectly.

They had grown up in the same village and had all the same mutual village friends. Unconcerned about their future, she was sure this was the way her life was designed—by his side, helping him become the man he was destined to be.

"It would be an understatement to say that you are my rock, Bella. You are my whole entire moon—and just like the earth, we are always in synchronous rotation with each other." He chuckled. "Corny, I know, it's just how you make me feel."

Bella blushed and gently pecked at his tiny nose. She covered every inch of his face with tiny kisses, and in that moment, she was utterly filled with passion and tenderness. "Right here, it's where we belong . . . I can't see me without you," he continued. Tucking her hair behind her ears to uncover her beautiful face, he was becoming everything to her, and she was already everything to him—the woman could have left a week ago and her scent would still remain on his pillow, a scent only he could recognize from within a crowd.

Natalie, the infamous village baker—her bakery consisting of more bread than any man could handle—was enticing and alluring. She could attract any man she wanted, and she did. As she baked her daily brioche, she sang and twirled, swirling the scent of her magnificent recipe out into the village streets. She had customers lined up outside the door. In that line, John, with an empty stomach, was famished. She had a thing for John, a good old-fashioned crush, but then again, who didn't? Eyeing him in the middle of the line, she gathered her most filling and most delicious selections and prepared a special bag just for him. Reaching over to the line, she handed him the bag and left off with a wink. She smiled and hurried behind the counter to finish tending to her line. John walked away with a slight grin, perplexed. The bread was devoured within minutes, and just as he was crumbling the paper bag to toss, he noticed something written on the side: her number. Suddenly, the idea of tossing this bag vanished, and he stuffed it in his back pocket and continued with his day. He'd never call her, he assured himself while envisioning Bella. Throughout the week, the thought of that phone number peeked through his mind more than a few times. *It ends with a four,* he thought. *No, maybe it's a two.* He'd check it just to end this game his mind was playing on him. *No harm in just checking,* he reasoned.

John had even considered maybe sending a quick little call to see if a bag like the one she had prepared him could be available again. There was no harm in being a hungry man. Why wouldn't a hungry man call the woman with the biggest Portuguese *papo secos* in the village? Bread rolls for the day—his mouth began to water.

He called. She gave him the bread, a little cheese, and even some coffee for the morning after. In his mind, he hadn't paid for it; he gave her nothing but pleasure in return. Rationalizing with himself, it was just a one-time thing.

Weeks had passed and a slight craving grew within him, a craving for some sweet, tasty bread. Bella would be busy this week. She's studying and had a full work schedule. Natalie wasn't sounding like an idea all that bad for the moment. He called. Arriving at her door, his hunger became dense and painful. She stood in the doorway half grinning, which was puzzling to him. He wondered what that facial expression meant. He didn't know if she was annoyed since it had been weeks or if she had the best of her best recipes waiting on the table for him inside. He followed behind her, deepening the hunger pains, and she teased with her hips. Lying on the table in front of him was something that swept the appetite clean from within him. It wasn't bread, coffee, cheese, or anything edible staring up at him. Instead, it was a deposit he had made from his last visit, the payment he believed he never left—the proof of a planted seed, a grain growing within her body, a baby croissant. She handed him the pregnancy test and smirked. "I hope you don't have alternate plans for your life," she joked.

Bella was John's only plan, his dream. Everything had been derailed. All he could do now was watch his hopes swirl down the drain, a drain of no return. This was the beginning of Bella's pain and the end of his love, a wreck of hearts for some Portuguese *papo secos*.

Sisters

Isn't it funny the way you can meet someone, have them briefly be a part of your life, yet their memory never dies no matter how much you wish it would?

There were three of us, each one beautiful in our own way. We never had it all, but we always had one another, and our mother always had a man. Some of them passive and hardly acknowledged us; others may have acknowledged us more than we'd like them to.

It was the day after Fourth of July when my mom had planned our beach day—she couldn't exactly afford to miss out on the holiday pay. The fifty-four-minute drive to the beach could've always gone in so many directions. On a few occasions, my older sister and I would really get into it over the fact that my sweaty thighs would rub against hers, and it never helped that the air conditioner was usually out of order.

We were about to experience our first time going anywhere with Robby—he was Mom's latest boyfriend. They began dating around winter. At first, he would come only at night while we were asleep. The comfortability grew, and he started staying in the mornings. We noticed someone else must have been around once we saw the extra breakfast place setting that was always taken to the bedroom once it was ready, but the biggest and most important difference we started to realize was that Mom seemed brighter. Her long days and nights at work were capped off when she was able to be beside him. I guess it never really mattered what type of guy he was as long as we knew Mom was better than she was before.

This day, Robby set the tone for us all. He was feeling great, which made my mother happy and, in turn, made us all feel quite jovial.

We spent the day in the water, carefree and limitless, splashing, floating, and creating this imaginative life where we were mermaids. Money wouldn't be an issue, men wouldn't come in and out, and we would live in the sun and be golden and beautiful for all our lives.

When they called us to shore, the laughter stopped and the imagination bubbles slowly drifted off into the horizon, following the sun as it lowered underwater.

We were treated to Popsicles on the breezy walk up to our car, each of us struggling to lick the Popsicle while trudging with a few of the beach items beside us. I was having a hard time keeping my eyes open since the salt from the water had filled behind them. I was anticipating the nice sleep I'd get in the car on the way home, and I was also anticipating how pissed my sister would be with my thighs against hers since, this time, it would be grainy, dirty, and dry.

We finished with our Popsicles by the time we reached the trunk, and we all left the items beside the car and made our way to the doors of the back seat. We had to wait. When Robby and my mother packed our items into the trunk, we climbed sleepily into the back, nesting our heads in the crevices of one another's shoulders. We knew there was no reason to bicker because we all needed one another to rest well. Thoughts and visions of seahorses, seashells, and pearls came in and then immediately out as I drifted off on this ride home.

When we got to the house moaning and groaning, all three of us had cricks in our necks and muscles that needed to be stretched out. This was when the bickering began. I yelled at my sister and told her how much I couldn't stand the stupid haircut she had gotten over the week, and she yelled back at me about how she wanted the bathing suit I was wearing—I forgot I had taken it from her drawer that morning. It's truthfully dreadful to argue with someone when you're wearing their clothes. It's like they could say "Shut up or give me my shit back." This continued back and forth for about three minutes while we continued to maneuver our way out of the car, but suddenly, we heard a loud slam. It was Robby, and he looked pissed. I had never seen his menacing eyes pierced in our direction and filled with anger. We were stunned and confused, and all six eyes peered in the direction of our mother, waiting for her to stop him in his tracks, but she continued up the stairs with our totes.

"If I have to hear any of you girls bitching any more, you're going to bed without eating shit." It was a long day of swimming with dolphins, so we were fucking hungry. We shut up, of course.

I thought about this for the entire night. I wondered why my mother didn't say anything. I wondered if she had asked him to start disciplining us. I had so many questions but even more sand in my ass, so I took a shower. In the shower, my questions continued, and I started to think even further as to how my sisters were feeling. Afterwards, we all ate dinner and made our way to bed that night, but for some time after, we walked on eggshells, fearful of the next time Robby might snap at us; and considering how he was comfortable enough to do it in front of Mom, it might happen at any moment.

Weeks followed, but it didn't happen. We were back to ourselves and had even forgotten what had happened during our last beach day.

It was September, and we were doing the routine back-to-school shopping with Mom. We were picking out undergarments, socks, and necessities. I told my mom how I thought I was ready to start wearing bikini-style underpants. I told her how my underwear was always showing above my jeans and how I was ready for the cuter brands. "I'm old enough," I said. She agreed to this and bought the cuter underwear for me, but still, I couldn't convince her to buy me a training bra. I would try again midyear.

I enjoyed days like this. We had lunch and shopped with Mom. We came home and laid all our clothes out on the bed, excited to mix and match the outfits. My older sister and I were about the same size, so we agreed to let each other swap out articles of clothing occasionally. Usually, agreements like this hardly stood up in the future.

I laid my clothes out for the next day, and the smell of Mom cooking spaghetti filled our bedroom. My mouth instantly watered. It was mainly the garlic bread I smelled.

I had hoped my sister would let me use her new pink sneakers to match the collared tee I picked out. She didn't, of course. Climbing onto my Native American–princess bedcovers on the bottom half of our bunk bed, I knew I had to ask her as kindly as I possibly could. "Could I borrow your—"
"Nope," she interrupted.

I drifted off to sleep and was sure the next thing I'd wake up to what would be the morning sun and the crisp imaginative smell of apples for the first day of school. Instead, it was Robby, slowly creaking the wooden bed frame and crawling to the center of my bed. I held my breath, waiting to see if this guy was sleepwalking. Maybe he was confused about whose bed this was; a sleepwalker could mistake a twin bunk for the queen bed he'd been sleeping in with my mother. When his arm began to slide up my thighs, I continued to give him the benefit of the doubt, assuming he was sleeping and dreaming I was my mother. I quickly flinched as if I were dreaming of the greatest mountain fall of all time. He must've woken and realized where he was because he immediately backed up and shut our door behind him. I initiated a fake trio sneeze, wondering if my sister was awake to bless me. She was snoring like warthog, sound asleep, and my heart was beating in my throat. *I'm sure that was an accident,* I assured myself and went back to sleep, attempting to resume the excitement for my first day.

The first day of school was a regular day, and it was like school just continued all summer with the same students and teachers from last year. All I could replay in my head was the old beer smell and scruffy, veiny arm on my thigh all coming from the man who finally put a smile on my mother's face. It was a logical excuse for someone to keep a secret like this to prevent my mom from yet another heartbreak. It was my very first severe secret, and I had no one I could talk to. For months, I kept it all inside, and it ate away at me every single day.

One day, in the late spring, we were drawing fake houses with chalk on our driveway pavement, and my youngest sister decided she was going to let Mom know her very first good boyfriend had been making her feel very uncomfortable with certain things he had been doing to her. The investigation was well under way before I could finally admit my awareness of all this, and I actually became so sick I threw up outside of the courtroom before the trial. An animated playback of all these events replayed in my head continuously, and all I could think of was the thing that must have triggered this all was that cuter, more mature underwear I had begged my mother to buy me.

Being a Woman

My Mother

Imagine if we were obligated to physically carry our struggles in a leather bag upon our backs, only then would we understand the burdens and the pains that others keep with them. I wonder, if that were the case, would we have more compassion towards others?

It would be astonishing to see how some children around us are carrying the heaviest of bags yet continue to walk so innocently and unchallenging.

Women carry so much more with them than what is in their purse. Our uterus and female reproductive organs alone have been more for us to carry than men since the beginning of time. We can get into the topic of carrying babies before and after they are born, their diaper bags and car seats—more things for us to carry.

What I have witnessed throughout the years has been just this, my mother carrying more weight than any man she has ever allowed into her life, mainly my father. I have seen a woman take on both roles effortlessly and carry the weight of the world upon her strong-willed back with not even so much as a request for a back rub.

They say that trauma, heartbreak, and pain make you stronger. Well, from the things I have seen in my life, I can vouch for that saying being authentic.

It is so easy to use these circumstances as an excuse, an excuse to become dependent on drugs and an excuse to live a life of failure.

For so many years, I had witnessed tears of uncertainty—not her uncertainty, but mine. She was always sure of the tears; she always fully understood the pain. It's something she could never erase, no matter how hard she'd try. I had no idea where the tears were coming from, and I was never sure how to approach the question of *why*.

Years later, I had accidentally discovered the answer. Everything changed the moment I had finally figured out the root of her pain. She did the best she could to harbor that memory. She did all she could to stay strong and ensure what happened to her would never happen to us. It didn't matter to the world what the events leading to her trauma were exactly; all that mattered was that she experienced it, and, my god, was she *resilient*. Now, I wonder if resilience is a genetic trait that we carry. I wonder if I inherited this from her.

I could never blame you for my issues. You've done nothing wrong; however, I could and will blame you for my strength and for my resilience. I blame you for my persistence and my heart. I 100 percent put all that blame on you. You have shown me what a real woman would do when faced with setbacks, hardships, bullshit, and trauma. You have shown me how to treat people—so kindly, so loving, and so tough.

I have prayed for you more times in my life than I have ever prayed for myself. I have prayed for you to continue to be the amazing woman you have shown the world you could be. I have prayed for you to continue to set an example for me and my child, to show us how hard work and dedication never goes unnoticed.

Everywhere I go, there is always someone reminding me how amazing you are. I couldn't imagine being the woman I am today without you leading the way. Never forget, your heart and soul have been so pure your entire life. I have seen you take in friends, family, and to me, strangers so no one had to live in the cold. I have witnessed your forgiving ways time and time again, only to allow others to continue their same hurtful behaviors towards you. I wondered how you could possibly resurrect yourself after so much damage. I wondered how you could still smile through it all. For years and years, it baffled me, and then . . . I became a mother.

It all started to become clear. Your perspective on life was to never give up because you were a mother. You saw your children, and the idea of failing made you cringe, so you always fought. No matter how tired, how sick, or how sad you felt, you never quit your job as a mother—never even took a fifteen. What a great mother you are. What a great person. I could never repay you enough. My only desire is to continue to make you proud.

Cotton, Fire, Silk

The curve of a woman's body is soft, perfect, and like nothing on this earth.

She comes in all different flavors. She comes in all different sizes.

Her touch can never be matched.

She touches with her hand but feels you with her heart.

Soft like cotton. Smooth like silk. Heated like fire.

The only sensations a man will always crave, whether it's in the form of the sweet or the bitter.

She always tastes so good.

All things sweet, honey, sugar, and butterscotch.

Enjoy her and rid her of her original flavor—love her 'til she's bitter.

First, she's soft, then she's smooth—handle her with care.

Fail to be fragile, now she's fire.

Cotton, fire, silk.

Walking Angel

I met a walking angel. She had the sweetest smile and a filtered halo, sparkling and shining above her head in real life. She was unblemished inside and out. She taught me to be forgiving and to see in the eyes of God. She taught me to love and see every situation as a path to things greater. So beautiful. So much kindness and purity. She'd be faced with hardships, and with tears falling, she'd smile and say, "This is my setup from God to bring me to higher." I never knew a person could understand all the people in this world and their actions that cause pain.

Forgiving. So very full of love. Enough love to feed the world. Enough compassion to end pain.

I have been so very blessed to walk with this angel. I have been so very blessed to witness such positivity. I love my walking angel.

Friend of My Soul

She was a friend of my soul because my person was constantly evolving—me as a human growing, grieving, creating, and learning—she was there through it all. It never mattered what phase I was going through, a friend was what she would always be.

Sometimes we forget what the true meaning of friendship can be represented as. We forget that a friend is the *love* of admiration. Colleague, acquaintance, associate, or buddy, whatever you want to call it, consider how many of these you have then really think about the number of *friends* you have, a friend who, after fifteen-plus years, has never invalidated your feelings and has never ignored your phone calls and a friend who has cried tears for you when you were too numb to cry yourself.

She was the friend of my soul because my entity had made mistakes. Despite the flaws and imperfections, she was a friend of my soul.

Consider the people in your life who are not only there for the situation but also celebrates your successes. Consider the people in your life who listen during a moment when it's really all you need, the friends who pull up on the hour you say you need them.

She was a friend of my soul because my human had suffered. During the darkest of times, I could depend on her to still see the real me.

So thankful for my soul friend.

His Wife

For as long as I have known you, you were the kind of girl that didn't need to touch a hot stove to know that it would burn. Your mother must have only had to warn you about the dangers of life just once. I would always think to myself how amazing your self-discipline and awareness were. You learned from the mistakes of those around you, and you never rushed through life trying to fit in. For you, it was always about what you were comfortable with, and you were not afraid to say when you did not want to be somewhere or do whatever the rest of the dumbass teenagers would be doing. I always loved that about you—you were very logical. In no way, shape, or form am I insinuating that you did not know how to have fun. You were the cool, smart one who, of course, made mistakes here and there but never anything that brought you down or held you back. When you met this man, you didn't jump right in just because he gave the kind of attention all the young girls would die for. You didn't develop feelings for him right away, because you knew what heartbreak looked like, and you knew what disrespect could do to a woman's self-esteem. You wouldn't allow anyone in unless you were sure they would never think to hurt your innocent, pure soul and body, a form of judgment most of us young females were pretty good at ignoring. Here is your story and what I've learned from you—thank you!

* * *

Holy shit, this bastard never changed his phone code. My heart begins to race as I slump behind the bathroom door. I reach up to feel the lock, making sure he couldn't come in and catch me if he just so happens to wake up. I'm swallowing golf balls every thirty seconds; I need water. I keep switching the hand in which I'm carrying the phone in because they are dripping with sweat. I'm afraid to look; I'm afraid he'll find out—but what the fuck? What if there is something for *me* to find out?

I've gained access, but he's snoring, and it's too late to bitch out now. First thing to snoop in, text messages—scrolling through, I see nothing. There's shit in his text messages— it's just me, his mom, and his boys. Bullshit, I know something's up—keep looking. Snap! Nothing—not even any newly added friends. I pretty much exhaust my brain looking through all his social media sources. I check his likes, comments, messages— there's not a damn thing for me to worry about. So why the hell have I been feeling so unsettled? Why is this gut-wrenching feeling still here? What do I have to do to calm my nerves and feel secure knowing he's literally not doing anything behind my back?

The click of the lock screen shutting down is loud. Oh man, I hope he didn't hear it. I try to silence the squeak of the bathroom door and the creak of the hardwood floors, and as softly as I possibly could, I reach the doorway to our bedroom and look over at him. He's sound asleep, faithfully and loyally sound asleep, and I am a crazy woman forever thinking otherwise.

I place his phone on the stand beside us and inch my way under the covers, my arm around his midsection. I snuggle up behind his neck to feel that comfort as I try to doze back off to sleep. My mind still hasn't calmed, but I keep trying to reassure myself there's nothing to worry about. *There's nothing to worry about*, I repeat in my head. Then *boom*, like a train, it hits me—his emails. Why didn't I check his emails? If I was going to search through his phone entirely for that reassurance, why didn't I check his emails? Why didn't I cover all grounds?

I jump out of bed. He's a heavy fucking sleeper, but I don't really give a shit. I snatch his phone off the stand and head back into the bathroom again. I shut the door and don't even bother locking it this time. I don't slump to the ground and contemplate shit; I enter the code and instantly click his emails. A bunch of emails from himself were the first thing to catch my eye. Why would he be sending all these emails to himself? I open the very first one, and it's a screenshot of a text message conversation. "Hey, babe, how is your day going?"—conversations so simple and considerate. He responses in detail of his day, how he is feeling, how he slept . . . (This bitch knows exactly how he sleeps—next to his wife!)

Now my heart is beating in my big toe, possibly a little in my ass too. I can't believe what I am reading right now. It's her, the same exact girl I've questioned him about, the girl who is "just a friend." I wondered so many times why the hell would he spend his lunch break with her when he could have easily met up with me.

I couldn't help but start to remember the beginning, when we were simply dating, when we're talking to someone—so much spark, so much excitement, the feeling of the butterflies, the thrill of stressing the kind of T-shirt I'd throw on to make a trip to the grocery store with him. Did all that die when I became his wife? Did he find that same type of excitement in her? I'm questioning in my head, *Why does she care so much about his day? Why did she spend most of her time interested in what he's been doing? Doesn't she know that it's my job to worry about all that?*

If I could explain in one word exactly how I'm feeling in this moment, I couldn't even fucking do that. I am sick to the core of my soul and ready to vomit all over this piece-of-shit phone. I make my second trip back to the bedroom, but this time, I couldn't give two shits less what kind of noise I'm making on my way. The floors are loud as fuck, the door is slammed open, and I wake up him up with the most unpleasant cell phone to the top of his hard-ass head. "Get the fuck up!" I scream as if the phone slamming against his head isn't enough for him to realize I'm fucking pissed. Of course, waking up to pain inflicted by the woman who loves you is all the reason to wake up angry yourself, but he had no chance against what I knew. I am furious and couldn't hold it in any longer—he ruined everything we had ever experienced together. "I gave you everything, and you spit in my fucking face—are you stupid?" At this point, any resistance I have inside of me to refrain from disrespect has gone out of the window. I am crying, yelling, cursing, slamming, and just exploding with sadness. "How could you do this to me?" Now I would love to explain his reaction, his answers, his expressions, but at this exact moment, I don't even see him, I don't hear him. My brain is screaming, and I cannot process real life. It's like I woke up from a bad dream that wasn't a dream at all. That fear and anxiety is confirmed—a nightmare come true.

* * *

That night was one of the worst feelings I had ever experienced. I felt like I was mourning the loss of a close loved one. And I was. I had lost the person I thought I knew, because deep down, I knew he was no longer a person I could trust the way I had all this time. Apologetic and self-pity were all I could read on his face the days that followed, battered and despondent. I couldn't bear to look at him for the way he made me feel and, more importantly, for the way I knew he was feeling.

I guess this is what we call unconditional love—a love so deep it doesn't even matter what he put me through.

Wait, you fucked around on me and I'm feeling sorry for you? The pain I feel for me becomes the pain you feel for me catching *you. Love so deep . . . the only thing I'm afraid of losing is you. Trust, pride, dignity—gone. Self, gone. You? But how could I handle losing you?*

For the next few following days, I found myself longing to be surrounded by friends, friends who would most likely understand his side over mine. I couldn't bear to hear anyone bashing his name with a meat cleaver. I'd be subconsciously begging them for his mercy, allowing me to vent my pains without them truly seeing it. For a moment, I began to make excuses, excuses for him and excuses for me, and reasons why I let this happened to me. I'd say, "Well, maybe I trusted him too much, I gave him all this freedom." His excuses would consist of the fact that I'd been bitchy lately— so of course, he'd find someone else to hear him out when he needed a friend—and that I was so consumed in my own issues lately.

I replayed the weeks leading up to these events repeatedly in my head, and I imagined myself being completely withdrawn. I had been on autopilot with him. I didn't even know it was possible to want to hold someone closer and tighter while, at the same time, feeling as though you want to suffocate them with a pillow during their phase of REM sleep. This was a pain I couldn't imagine healing from, and my best option, as I saw it, would be to simply forget. Over the years, we had shared everything together, and I was at least under this impression; in fact, he had even uttered those words once.

It was a late summer evening in July, and we had stayed out in Newport for his brother's wedding. Carrying my heels through the lobby of the hotel, the imprint of the strap tattooed in red ink on my skin, I was mumbling since I slightly overdid the vodka.

"I forgot my toothbrush." I laughed. I joked about my morning breath mixed with the liquor and even the chance of me vomiting before the end of the night. Looking back at him as he steadily and firmly grabbed my hand, assisting me with my balance, I see him he smile. It was my favorite thing to look at. Running his fingers through my stiff, hairspray-filled hair, he kissed me, a soft purposeful kiss. He knew he was about to say something that would instantly take my breath away. "I have my toothbrush, babe, and for the rest of our lives, we share everything." The insensitive side of me had taken a leave of absence with him, gone for good. In my past, I'd immediately gag in disgust—the thought of sharing a toothbrush with someone—but me now, I knew he literally couldn't have said anything better than this.

The rest of that night was beautiful. We made the most amazing love and pinky swore tons of promises for all the remaining days.

I am usually terrible at remembering things, but of course, when I'm feeling extremely pained and down, why wouldn't I remember something to hammer the nail in my coffin?

I called him a late Tuesday evening to see if he'd be interested in meeting up to further discuss some questions I simply had to ask. The little devil on my left shoulder had me with pen and paper in hand, ready to ask all the nitty-gritty shit I knew I did *not* need and want to know. Meanwhile, the little angel sat with her head hung, for she knew there wasn't a thing she could say to stop me from pestering him about these details.

That evening, discussing things over hot tea since it was the only thing I could keep down, we sat wide-eyed, neither of us sure where to begin.

"Where did it all begin?" I croaked. The tears were working their way up in the back of my fucking head, and I couldn't let him have any more power over me. I heard if you stare up at a light when the tears roll up, it stops them from falling. It was worth a shot. I looked up, stared as hard as I could at the bright-ass lights above me. Still, the pain I felt in my chest screamed and begged to release them. Waterfalls. He knew he was still my end all and be all. I had given so much of this to God. I told God I knew now this lesson was for me to never put anyone on a pedestal so high—what a terrible place to be anyway. There was only one way off, and that's down, and that's exactly the direction he was headed.

I demanded every single day and play-by-play of how and why this had all gone the way it did. That's exactly what he gave me as I pushed the vomit back down my esophagus with a slurp of my hot tea, which had now grown cold. This was more than an affair; it was a relationship. Even worse, it was a friendship that had grown more important than our marriage. I wanted this bitch to feel this hurt. I wanted her head. I'm not fighter, but here I was imagining myself bashing her brains in.

If ever there was a time in my life where I felt like I needed to find forgiveness within myself and those around me, it was now. This was the hardest hurdle I've ever had to climb in my life. I was allowing this anger to swallow me whole and take over all my relationships, including my relationship with God. The way I had decided to forgive him had been contingent upon the ways I had believed God wanted me to forgive him. With hindsight, I should have never allowed the friendship to happen, but I do not blame myself for being so trusting. I've done all I could have done, and I've accepted the fact that this mistake was no longer mine to fix; it was all on him. I may have learned a few things from this occurrence; however, he was the one who truly had a lesson to learn, and by the way he appeared, he seemed to have felt entirely accountable for my pain.

I believe in second chances, and I now know that if this were to happen again, I am ready to accept this fate and move forward with my life. What was important for me to remember was that we shared everything, and that meant pain, guilt, sorrow, and all things unpleasant. I still wanted to share everything with him. And I did.

Dear Au-some Mom

Everyone talks about the differences of your child between other typical children. They talk about the difficulties, the hardships, the pain, and the fear. They never talk about the moms—the moms that toughen up when they realize their child has a chance, the moms who know their child deserves the best treatment and services, and the moms who refuse to stop until their child can live with less frustration and less sadness.

I'd like to praise the mothers who dig in the soil and get their hands dirty just to find the resources needed for more smiles on their child's face throughout the day. You have shown me that if we were advocates for our children, if we had faith for our children, we would see progress. Tears have discreetly filled my eyes watching your expressions with every step of progress made by your child. My heart explodes the moment I see your happiness watching your child laugh and play.

I have the pleasure of experiencing true warriors battling for their children on a day-to-day basis. I have been around during some of your most difficult moments and meltdowns but equally around for your happiest and proudest. There have been times where you were running on below-zero energy, driving on autopilot fulfilling the needs of your family, tending to their wants and essentials. For me to say you advocated would be an understatement; you are the MLK for your child. Shield and armor to bed, your child blocks his ears to the loud noises, and you block your ears to the doubtful hope they give you. You believe in yourself, you believe in your child, and most of all, you believe in the fight. Your child is so unique, and you are so strong. What a pleasure it has been to work with you. You have showed me what it truly means to be a fighting mom.

Au-some mom, you are so different, you are so unique, and you are so made for this.

Keep fighting!

Rapunzel

Do you know that story of the girl named Rapunzel, the beautiful princess who had been trapped in a tower for years and years, secluded from the outside world? Rapunzel was taken away from her family and friends by an evil character who had manipulated her into believing she had no one else but him. She was the girl who supposedly threw her beautiful long hair down to the prince charming waiting to save her on the safe ground below. Well, her friends never knew if she was okay or if she was happy; they never even knew if she was still up there. Until one day, she showed up to an evening for the girls out in the town. That night, it was clear that all that time, she was not okay, and the rumors were false because there never was a prince charming.

One night while reading poetry in her bedroom, Rapunzel realized that although she was so accustomed to this life, so used to being away from the spotlight, she was growing to resent the walls in which she lived in. Rapunzel decided there was no way in hell she would continue to live this way. On that night, Rapunzel took a deep breath and leaped to freedom, unharmed and ready to begin living her best life.

Rapunzel had lived one way for so long, how difficult it was to change it all around with one decision in one day. I am marveled by her courage and strong desire to go out and attain better.

* * *

You wonder, at what age do we begin to become the person we will always be? Will there ever be a specific time, or do we evolve into that person slowly, maintaining the mannerisms we have had since birth? Lucky for me, I am almost positive to have that answer, and I can thank my memory for that. I can take a person in my life, and so long as they've been in my life long enough, I analyze my memories of this person since a very young age. How does their young personality compare to the soul they have become today?

This one is for you:

I can remember you in grade school. There was never a time during our friendship where I felt you did not appear to be flawless. You've always known the power of your beauty and, more importantly, the magic of your heart. There have been times throughout the years when you may have allowed another person, or even multiple people, stray your mind from the acceptance of yourself. You may have been put down during times you were mentally incapable of maintaining your appearance.

Nonetheless, you were still beautiful.

You never looked down from the pedestal in which you placed your heart. You always knew that placing it higher than anyone could ever reach was exactly where it belonged. You never forgot your intentions; you remained pure and true. You were always torn between what you knew you were worth and the worth you were willing to be accepted for.

If he craved your heart, it would be bleeding in your hand with a silk bow on top.

I wondered how many times you'd stay in the tower just to hide the bruises. I wondered if you'd ever be able to leave. I remember even wondering if you'd survive.

I remember constantly wondering if you would rationalize and figure out your true value, wondering if there would be a point in time when you would finally run from it all. I wanted to remind you every day how beautiful, smart, and kindhearted you were, because I knew you needed to hear it from someone who truly loved you.

I understand that you never wanted to be around your friends. I understand that you never wanted anyone to see you that way, never wanted anyone to hear the way your phone goes off when you're not around him.

I never passed judgment on you; I simply prayed.

There were no stairs, elevators, or ladders to this tower, so I knew the day that you jumped, you meant it. I could not have been happier for you.

I was wrong. I could be happier for you, and as the weeks and months passed, when I came to realize that you had completely forgotten that the tower had even existed, my happiness increased immensely.

Everyone has a Rapunzel or two in their lives, and she is stunning, strong, and she carries the kindest heart of them all. Despite what she believes she is worth, what she believes she deserves, there is so much more to her than the tower she lives in. We can only hope that one day, she decides to jump and save herself.

Senseless

How many times do you have to hear from the people around you how senseless you are until you finally start to realize it? This is usually the case when you're in love with the wrong person. Everything they do, good or bad, just always makes sense to you after an explanation is provided, even if it's just one word. Before the explanation, and in the heat of the moment, you're so angry, and this is seriously the last straw. You swear on everything.

The text message of fuel is delivered, and you're ready to battle the blaze, but the response isn't fire; it's calm and oh so believable, and there you are again—bowing, crawling on your knees, simply submissive.

* * *

Dear Roxanne,

I have watched you firsthand exemplify the phrase "love is blind." My dear, you were terribly, hopelessly blind—oblivious to so many things—and no one could help you see it at all. I remember you bawling in tears, feeling so deserted by everyone around you, alienated for putting so much hope into your relationship that noticeably could never work. Not one person agreed to your choices. For lack of a better word, they called you stupid, and as much as I love you, I could not have agreed anymore.

You were a teenager when you fell in love with him, and your whole world shifted in that moment. He became your whole pie plus the whipped-cream topping, and I must add, the whipped cream was artificial.

Whenever we invited you to dinner, to bowling, or simply just to hang out in one of our cars, you'd first have to make sure he had alternative plans. If there was even a slim chance he did not have plans, he could possibly get bored and maybe want to spend time playing videos game in your presence. With a possibility like that, our offer would completely be avoided. No one had the heart to tell you what it really was, and I guess we just figured you'd find out sooner or later. The reality of it was when things were good between the two of you, they were great. And happy really looked so beautiful on you—your eyes twinkled, your smile shined, and your skin even reflected the great feelings inside that you must have been feeling. What kind of friends would we have been to interrupt that? We loved to see you glowing. When all that joy and radiance dwindled down and the spark died, you were gray—frizzy and dry. We'd jump in with all sorts of tips and hints as to why we believe he's hurting you from the sidelines. You'd never listen; all you were focused on was how to mend the momentary disagreements, how you could look and feel beautiful and happy again. How could I blame you? Aren't we all looking for this feeling? Searching in the wrong places for the instant high of endorphins, just waiting on that someone who makes us feel so worthy in a world where we are simply one of billions?

Back then, there were so many times when you couldn't join us to hang out, and it was then when we spoke. We spoke and spoke of all the ways he'd abused you although never physically. "We'd never ever be able to deal with such bullshit," we'd say. "You're such a dumbass. His penis must be made of gold," we'd joke. "What could we do to help her?" some of us would ask. And the rest of us would just say, "Let her find out for herself." What good would we be doing you by telling you something you would never believe, telling you something that wouldn't change how you felt about him but would change how you felt about us? There was no hope.

Believe it or not, years had gone by before you ever really began to see it, before you ever even started to consider the chance of him not being the one for you. It was then we were able to finally knock some sense into you, let you know about the women he was willing to kick it to on the side had they not known he was in a relationship with you. All he had to do was feed you lies and love notes, and you'd forget it all. It was always questionable as to whether he truly loved you. Did he see you the way your friends did? We saw all the good in you—the pureness of your heart and the kind manner of your soul. If he did, why hurt someone so worthy? Something none of us had known was that you always saw things for what they were. You knew of all the dirt, grime, and filth. You knew the kind of man he was out in the open behind your back, but what you held on to was the man he was behind closed doors with you. What it meant to you when he told you he loved you and the way he'd look into your eyes when he said it—you knew his heart, and you knew he meant it. No, of course you knew it wasn't okay for him to do that to you. You knew he wouldn't change right away, and you knew it would take time. What you knew from deep within was far greater than what any of us could have learned; you saw people for who they were and not their actions. We called you stupid, we called you senseless, but you were never any of those things. In fact, we were ignorant to your truth. You forgave countlessly because he was not made of his actions, and you had truly grown a love for him. A love so strong that it could do nothing more than to stick around for the lessons of life; it yearned to heal and help the individuals who needed it. His story had falls, breakdowns, and pain, and you listened to it all and understood that what he'd been through had caused him to act the way he'd been acting. You cradled him in your hands because you truly believed you had the power to heal. And you did. It may have taken some time, but yes, you did heal; and you may not have come out on top with this one because you were left in pain, but, my friend, you helped someone by sticking around through the hardships. You believed in someone when no one else did, and you understood for the greater good that hurting and being hurt is growth for the both of you. For that, I am so proud of you.

The Flower

In the summer, you shine. After a long day of sitting under the sun, when the heat from your core starts to cool off, your skin peels yellow flower petals and you glow. The gold reflection on your body radiates a soul so pure, comparable to the stem of a sunflower—rough around the edges while the central being is beautiful. Are there any mirrors around you? Do you see how many people would pick you? Hair, skin, smile, and soul—everything gold. You are your best self around this time of year, and they all want to be surrounded by your soft look and rugged personality.

You could have anyone, and you wanted no one.

You could have danced in the sun, but you decided to wait for the moonlight instead.

They wanted to hydrate you in water, but you chose cognac. After all, it gave you that happy bronzed appearance and that I-could-give-a-shit-less attitude too.

People would come to the field after the drop of the sun. They moved with you but never to your rhythm.

They'd sense your strength connected to your roots, and intimidated, they'd walk away.

These people could make you laugh, and they could make you cry, but they could never pull you from the soil.

They never knew, once upon a time, you had been pulled from the ground. You were lifted and in love. Your petals were constantly wilting and removed. "He loves me not" was much of the theme at each loss of a petal.

The frail hope of "he loves me" petals clinging to dear life, tears falling down so silently—you were thrown to the ground.

With each tear feeding your roots, you replanted yourself, stronger, deeper, and more fearless. Never worried about being "picked" again.

The wonderful part of your story is that you now know all your petals scream "I love me."

The Bath

It all started in the bathtub. I laid my head against the edge of the tub and let my eyes fall upon my huge stomach. Pain overcame me in a way it had never overcame me before, and I began to weep. I've always wanted to be a mother. I remember saying I couldn't wait to have kids when I was just eleven years old. Here I am, months away from becoming a mother, and I couldn't be any more terrified. The birth, the parenting, the pain—yes, all that scared me, but what scared me the most was this feeling of being terminally ill.

I felt like the moment I was told I was going to have a child; the doctor added a disclaimer that noted, "You also are going to die at the hands of this man. He is going to fucking kill you, and there is no way out."

I just wished that God would beat him to it. Take me away before he does.

Maybe if I die giving birth, I thought to myself, *I won't have to meet my precious child. I won't feel any pain leaving her behind. Maybe if I die giving birth, she will never know the amount of love I can shower her with. She wouldn't feel a loss. She would never know how silly I used to be, and she would never get to be embarrassed by me in front of her friends. We would never have lunch dates together, and we would never cuddle on a movie night at home. She would never know.*

"I hope I fucking die in the delivery room!" I screamed. I meant it. I truly, honestly meant it. It was my passive way of suicidal thoughts.

"Please, Lord, let me die while bringing this wonderful new life into this world," I begged with him; I made deals.

I didn't die.

I am so thankful I didn't die.

Instead, I was reborn. I was a mother. I never want to leave this little angel, and I never want her to leave me.

At a point in my life where I had lost faith in life. I had lost faith in ever feeling happiness and joy ever again, but I gave birth to it. She became all things joyful—she even brought joy to strangers.

It ended in the bathtub. A splashing, beautiful, vibrant baby full of love, laughter, and expression.

A love so deep that had I ever left this earth without experiencing it, I would have never truly even lived.

Stepmom

There isn't much to be said when a person is destructive. It may seem like they know what they're doing, but in most cases, they have no idea. They're like tornados with no control of their actions, whirling everyone and everything into their mess, swinging them and throwing them out on their asses. It's impossible to stop. You can get out of their way, avoid their path, and still they will find a way to involve you in their clutter.

Having to deal with someone like this in your family is like a glass-infested horse pill going down without any liquids. A person who once was a pleasure to have around becomes the person everyone hopes would maybe catch a flat tire on the way to the most recent family function. Deep down inside, we all want this person to be who they were before, go back to their old ways, because, quite frankly, there's nothing good about their new self.

Only a doctor could perform a diagnosis, and I'm sure there were some unnatural things going on. It's a grieving process for all involved, including the person suffering. We grow in healthy ways, and sometimes we grow apart from ourselves and others we love. With this process, everyone is learning and adjusting. We are all trying to be supportive while the sufferer is trying to not suffer. We become obsessed with fixing this person and helping them come to their senses so much that, in time, we begin to feel more disappointment than anything. What we forget a lot of the time is that people are going to do what they are going to do. There are so many actions and behaviors of others that spiral out of our control. *Out* of our control. This means there is *nothing* we can do about it. We are so tough on ourselves, blaming ourselves for allowing our loved ones to reach this point.

We all have our own paths and journeys—be it your mother, child, sibling, or loved one. This life is an individual opportunity, and we are set to walk our own paths. Once these paths become intertwined, the person stumbling along theirs will bring you down with them. Send love, send support, and send advice. Do whatever you feel you must do in order to contribute your greatest level of assistance *without* joining them on their path.

Full Circle

Stop stressing about the people that stress you. Understand this: life comes full circle. Do good and be good, and good will come your way. Do not fall under the trap of petty revenge; the cycle will never end. People will hurt you, so let them. People will act out, and their behaviors will be irrational and unfair. Let them. They are out of your control. Life comes full circle. They will lie in the beds they make and barely sleep well again. It is out of our controls to try to mold and shape people who are beyond repair. We pain ourselves trying. We take things personally and seek out the ever-so-trending word of *pettiness*. The man cheats; she burns his shit. The man is cheated on; he beats her. We react and so does the universe. Allow those to make their mistakes and let karma be their instructor. Stop using people as your mirror. Their poor actions and choices are not a reflection of you. Be your own beautiful image—be good!

Ugly Duckling

I've always felt like the ugly duckling straight out of the children's story—different and could never easily blend in. Some days I'd embrace it and love the skin I was in and love the brain I had been blessed with. Other days, I'd wonder how or why I was nothing like those around me. I had assumed that being different was equivalent to being set apart from the rest—a negative, terrible thing to be, different. I never stopped to consider the possibility of its meaning simply that I could and should stand out. I was afraid of being myself, afraid of speaking my own voice because, of course, my opinion differed from the rest. People hardly agreed. My differences, disagreements, and uncomfortable nature in any happy setting for you all threw me into a temporary sadness.

Over time, I began to realize my differences were beautiful. I loved me. I embraced me. I'd hear them say "She thinks she's better"—this is a wonderful thing to think of me. I never thought I was better than anyone, just only better than myself yesterday, loving and accepting my unique mind-set. Such a beautiful thing being the ugly duckling. They usually turn into swans.

Shit for Lunch

How could I ever feel hungry when I was so full of fear?

A little bowl of threats for breakfast.

A beautiful garden salad tossed in abuse and an ingredient called low self-esteem ho.

A savory dinner baked with a little bit of too much fucking care.

"You're so skinny."

"Why don't you eat?"

"I could see your bones."

I was being fed bullshit daily.

My friends and family all see my body suffering, but of course, it has to be postpartum.

I'm telepathically screaming to my sister at the table, but we just don't have the connection.

My mother tells me she's afraid I might vanish.

My brother jokingly calls me a skinny bitch.

My bracelets slide off and get lost in my oversized sleeves.

I promise you, I could hear my tailbone click against the seats every time I sit down.

Every word I hear, I roll it into this little ball of hatred for myself. I keep it in my back pocket. I set a daily reminder on my phone to announce "Yes, I am that dumbass bitch."

Some women can only hide their pain for so long.

And a man like this loves when it shows.

"I'll take extra care of you, baby, I know you haven't been yourself.

"You don't need your friends and family judging us, baby, stay here with me."

One hot summer day in August, I fought. I prayed and stood the fuck up for myself.

Here and now, I lick the bones of the tender red meat I like to call revenge. I smile at the Lord for giving me the strength.

I eat! My watch fits, my ass jiggles, and I feel so free!

I have grown such an impactful love for myself. My hunger for peace is never-ending. My thirst for positivity is powerful. My resilience radiates phenomenally.

Thank you so much for backing the fuck up so I could take the time to love *me*!

The Blindfold

Abuse usually comes with a ten-pack of blindfolds—one for the abuser, the victim, her family, and her friends. The blind eye becomes just as dominant as him. We never see the marks because we believe every excuse. We ignore the disrespectful comments because this is what couples do. She barely comes around anymore, and it's cool, we'll open gifts without her. "She's in love." We all giggle. "He must really be good to her."

Overtime these blindfolds begin to become part of our faces, and we see nothing wrong here. Even on the day she finally couldn't hide it, we turn a cheek to the madness because she survived it. We say, "Let her do what she wants if that's where she wants to say." Wide-eyed when she says she loves him, we literally just look the other way. The blindfolds come off, so we all see what's going on; she's naked without it, so she puts it back on. You literally feel like there's not much you can do when a girl's blindfold becomes a part of her face, her identity.

Being a Man

Selfish

Twenty-three minutes until we reach our destination, seventeen minutes since the last word either of us have spoken—not that we were loud or obnoxious in conversation, it's just unclear as to which of us had been heard. She's shaken, uneasy, afraid, and quite frankly, alone. Though I am sitting right beside her, she refuses to acknowledge my presence any longer.

She must've forgotten to apply lotion on her hands today, and the brisk morning air attacked her skin like minirazors. The coffee-brown nail polish had chipped on her thumbnails and had completely chiseled from her right index finger. She's gripping her purse as if it contains her whole life inside when there are just used makeup tissues and a small can of Lysol. I know, I was looking for a lighter a few days earlier.

I assume I'm supposed to feel regretful for the way I've been acting, yet that feeling is something unfamiliar to me. Maybe she is waiting for me to utter the perfect words that would settle her stomach, and yet I have no urge to speak.

To be in the mind of a woman is something I have no interest in exploring. Truthfully, I don't even want to ask her if she would like a refreshment from the gas station I plan to stop at. She may continue to resent me or even forget my existence, and this is something I am perfectly comfortable with. In fact, it is something I much rather prefer.

Despite her physical beauty, intriguing mind, and ability to make me feel like I am the only man she'd ever met, I am not ready to father her child. The decision she wants to make on the organism growing within her is not my concern.

The Rooftop

It was always an amazing feeling the moment you tell me you were heading to get me. I had no idea an adventurous side of me had even existed until you'd occasionally tempt it to come out and play. Those two words you'd text me—*get ready*—and I'd immediately oblige. This one specific night, it was as if the stars had waited and practiced all month to shine the way they did. They must have sent you an invitation because you knew exactly where we needed to be when the sun fell. You picked me up and escorted me back to your place. I looked over at you in discouragement; I didn't want to be just another object for your sexual desires. Your knowing smile encouraged me to rest assured this was something great. We tiptoed through the dark, cold house; the central air covered your home, and I hated to be cold. You brought me upstairs and grabbed a few comforters, then we creeped out the second-floor window and up onto the rooftop. Grasping my hand behind you, you looked back at me and smirked.

It was the same outdoor view we had just come in from, but I felt as though I had stepped into a whole new world. The stars were more than breathtaking—they were life-changing. I couldn't remember if I had ever told you how much the stars meant to me. I don't know if you've done this before; all I knew was this was a moment I will never forget. The time stood still as we lay there on your rooftop, talking until the stars waited for an encore. The sun began to rise, and all I could do was hope you would bring me here again someday.

I fell in love with your simple ways; after all, I was the simplest complicated girl to deal with ever. What a good feeling to feel, as though someone genuinely wanted to see you enjoy the things you loved. You'd pick me up and do random things like this all the time, and I continued to fall for you. You showed me how fun doing nothing with someone who matched your soul could be. You showed me how to feel special with the smallest acts of love, yet you never uttered those words. I never thought I'd be a "What are we?" type of girl, but right now, it was the only thing I could question. Forehead kisses and playing with my hair, falling asleep with your head buried in my curls—it baffled me how you just weren't head over heels in love with me yet. When we were high, I would be your first pick when any type of formal event would come up, and I would be the last person you text at night. It was a roller-coaster ride with you. Butterflies consumed me with each drop-in communication. You'd sometimes go days without checking in on me, without wanting to see me. I'd wash my hair every day just waiting for the day you'd ask to feel it on your skin, and I'd want that tropical scent to be strong enough to put you to sleep the moment you'd lay beside me.

In and out, month after month, you knew how to keep me wanting more. We were in a real shituation. Just when I'd tell myself I'm over you and I'm over your games, you'd make me swoon so easily once again. I'd block you and unblock you. I'd think about your laugh and then imagine me knocking your teeth in. Beyond a crush and less than love, what do we even call this shit, and what's the remedy to get the fuck over it?

Right Person vs. Wrong Time

Ever wonder how someone could be perfect for you in every sense, but the only thing is the timing is off? You'll experience the best of times with them, and almost every time you're with them is a great time. They have almost every quality you seek in a person, except the ability to commit. It's like you're being teased with a piece of meat—someone's dangling it right in front of you and it smells good, looks good, and let's admit it, you're hungry. Each time you try to reach for it, you're given the excuse of "it's not a good time for me."

Time will always be against us. For once, let's just fight back.

Songs

There are certain songs that get me going, the kind of songs that bring a flash of an entire season sliding across the front of my mind all within a second. The type of feel-good song that doesn't just bring me to my feet but balances me on the very point of my big toes. They raise the hairs, bumps, and skin altogether, still and stiff like Black Ice gel. A song that will repeat the same chorus four times in three minutes but will replay an entire relationship in my head—a relationship that *could* have been.

Ultimately, it's more than just a song; it's the strawberry Frutista I sipped every night after the sixteen-minute wait in the Taco Bell drive-through.

With just one sip, and every moment after, the smell of his aftershave danced around in the back of my throat. I start to wonder what it is about him that gets me so high, that makes me so addicted to his presence. After all, his barber could have done a better job on his beard lining; it is never quite straight enough for me. I have maybe once or twice question the fact that he listens to Amy Winehouse. I have my suspicions on his sexuality. Let's not forget the way he skins and eats apples—it is like watching a toddler learning to use his new molars.

I could write a list of all his flaws and still crave the feeling of his fingertips simply holding the bottom of my chin. In this moment, he would call attention to my annoying perfectionist tendencies. I would feel like a student, subject to the way he teaches me everything I need and didn't know about myself, looking from the outside in. I am a submissive by nature, and I need to be directed, and to me, that means far from being controlled and it means having a life partner there to help guide the way for success all while achieving his own, the way he would acknowledge my passions, light their wicks, and allow them to explode like fireworks during the first week of July.

I am constantly aware of my soul, and it is hungry for a man of his kind, a man that not only sets my soul on fire but one who could extinguish the flames and soothe the burn.

Seasons

Rare Case

All this information on abuse and mistreatment—it has been said that people do not change, and I can never agree with this phrase. I have witnessed people remain stagnant in their negative ways for years. I have also witnessed rare cases where someone goes from a winter blizzard straight to a beautiful, easy summer day—certainly not easy, but very possible. This person relentlessly came through the storms day in and day out. It was difficult to deal with, hard to live with, and debilitated those in their path. It was a never-ending case of seeking means of survival in this storm. Provided with consequence and resources, this person equally was relentless in stopping their self-destruction. And it happened. It happened one step at a time; the cars were dug out, and life started to move around. The snow began to melt, and the grass began to grow. The sun found its way to shine, and this person became different. Persistence, help, resources, mental-health assistance—everything this person could use in order to be better, they did, and they did it with purpose.

Never let anyone tell you that a person can't change. You need to introduce the resources and provide them with affirmation and positive support, but let them go and heal. Let them go and watch them grow.

CPSIA information can be obtained
at www.ICGtesting.com
Printed in the USA
LVHW091325100519
617404LV00001B/90/P